WORLD'S BEST SHORT STORIES

GP EDITORS

GENERAL PRESS

Published by
GENERAL PRESS
4805/24, Fourth Floor, Krishna House
Ansari Road, Daryaganj, New Delhi - 110002
Ph : 011-23282971, 45795759
E-mail : generalpressindia@gmail.com

www.generalpress.in

First Edition : 2022

ISBN : 9789354992278

Published by Azeem Ahmad Khan for General Press

BESTSELLING FICTION

- 1984 by George Orwell
  Literature & Fiction, ISBN: 9789380914947

- A Passage to India by E.M. Forster
  Literature & Fiction, ISBN: 9789354990205

- A Room of One's Own by Virginia Woolf
  Literature & Fiction, ISBN: 9789354990281

- A Wrinkle in Time by Madeleine L'Engle
  Literature & Fiction, ISBN: 9789354991066

- Animal Farm by George Orwell
  Literature & Fiction, ISBN: 9789380914701

- Anthem by Ayn Rand
  Literature & Fiction, ISBN: 9789389157079

- As a Man Thinketh by James Allen
  Literature & Fiction, ISBN: 9788180320262

- As I Lay Dying by William Faulkner
  Literature & Fiction, ISBN: 9789390492381

- Demian by Hermann Hesse
  Literature & Fiction, ISBN: 9789387669567

- Lost Horizon by James Hilton
  Literature & Fiction, ISBN: 9789389716313

- Mansarover 1 (Hindi) by Premchand
  Literature & Fiction, ISBN: 9789380914978

- One, None and a Hundred Thousand by Luigi Pirandello
  Literature & Fiction, ISBN: 9789389716337

Search the book by its ISBN

BESTSELLING FICTION

- Siddhartha by Hermann Hesse
  Literature & Fiction, ISBN: 9789380914145

- Tales from Shakespeare by Charles Lamb & Mary Lamb
  Literature & Fiction, ISBN: 9789380914367

- The Mysterious Affair at Styles by Agatha Christie
  Literature & Fiction, ISBN: 9789390492510

- The Plague by Albert Camus
  Literature & Fiction, ISBN: 9788194764892

- The Prophet by Kahlil Gibran
  Literature & Fiction, ISBN: 9789380914022

- The Railway Children by E Nesbit
  Literature & Fiction, ISBN: 9789354990960

- The Sound and the Fury by William Faulkner
  Literature & Fiction, ISBN: 9789390492572

- The Stranger by Albert Camus
  Literature & Fiction, ISBN: 9789390492589

- The Sun Also Rises by Ernest Hemingway
  Literature & Fiction, ISBN: 9789354990984

- Their Eyes Were Watching God by Zora Neale Hurston
  Literature & Fiction, ISBN: 9788194764885

- To the Lighthouse by Virginia Woolf
  Literature & Fiction, ISBN: 9789390492190

- World's Best Short Stories: Volume 1 by Various Authors
  Literature & Fiction, ISBN: 9789390492275

Search the book by its ISBN

Contents

STORY 1
THE PRINCESS

DH Lawrence

To her father, she was The Princess. To her Boston aunts and uncles she was just *Dollie Urquhart, poor little thing.*

Colin Urquhart was just a bit mad. He was of an old Scottish family, and he claimed royal blood. The blood of Scottish kings flowed in his veins. On this point, his American relatives said, he was just a bit "off". They could not bear any more to be told *which* royal blood of Scotland blued his veins. The whole thing was rather ridiculous, and a sore point. The only fact they remembered was that it was not Stuart.

He was a handsome man, with a wide-open blue eye that seemed sometimes to be looking at nothing, soft black hair brushed rather low on his low, broad brow, and a very attractive body. Add to this a most beautiful speaking voice, usually rather hushed and diffident, but sometimes resonant and powerful like bronze, and you have the sum of his charms. He looked like some old Celtic hero. He looked as if he should have worn a greyish kilt and a sporran, and shown his knees. His voice came direct out of the hushed Ossianic past.

For the rest, he was one of those gentlemen of sufficient but not excessive means who fifty years ago wandered vaguely about, never arriving anywhere, never doing anything, and never definitely being anything, yet well received in the good society of more than one country.

He did not marry till he was nearly forty, and then it was a wealthy Miss Prescott, from New England. Hannah Prescott at twenty-two was fascinated by the man with the soft black hair not yet touched by grey, and the wide, rather vague blue eyes.

Many women had been fascinated before her. But Colin Urquhart, by his very vagueness, had avoided any decisive connection.

Mrs. Urquhart lived three years in the mist and glamour of her husband's presence. And then it broke her. It was like living with a fascinating spectre. About most things he was completely, even ghostly oblivious. He was always charming, courteous, perfectly gracious in that hushed, musical voice of his. But absent. When all came to all, he just wasn't there. "Not all there," as the vulgar say.

He was the father of the little girl she bore at the end of the first year. But this did not substantiate him the more. His very beauty and his haunting musical quality became dreadful to her after the first few months. The strange echo: he was like a living echo! His very flesh, when you touched it, did not seem quite the flesh of a real man.

Perhaps it was that he was a little bit mad. She thought it definitely the night her baby was born.

"Ah, so my little princess has come at last!" he said, in his throaty, singing Celtic voice, like a glad chant, swaying absorbed.

It was a tiny, frail baby, with wide, amazed blue eyes. They christened it Mary Henrietta. She called the little thing *My Dollie.* He called it always *My Princess.*

It was useless to fly at him. He just opened his wide blue eyes wider, and took a child-like, silent dignity there was no getting past.

Hannah Prescott had never been robust. She had no great desire to live. So when the baby was two years old she suddenly died.

The Prescotts felt a deep but unadmitted resentment against Colin Urquhart. They said he was selfish. Therefore they discontinued Hannah's income, a month after her burial in Florence, after they had urged the father to give the child over to them, and he had courteously, musically, but quite finally refused. He treated the Prescotts as if they were not of his world, not realities to him: just casual phenomena, or gramophones, talking-machines that had to be answered. He answered them. But of their actual existence he was never once aware.

They debated having him certified unsuitable to be guardian of his own child. But that would have created a scandal. So they did the simplest thing, after all – washed their hands of him. But they wrote scrupulously to the child, and sent her modest presents of money at Christmas, and on the anniversary of the death of her mother.

To The Princess her Boston relatives were for many years just a nominal reality. She lived with her father, and he travelled continually, though in a modest way, living on his moderate income. And never going to America. The child changed nurses all the time. In Italy it was a Contadina; in India she had an ayah; in Germany she had a yellow-haired peasant girl.

Father and child were inseparable. He was not a recluse. Wherever he went he was to be seen paying formal calls going out to luncheon or to tea, rarely to dinner. And always with the child. People called her Princess Urquhart, as if that were her christened name.

She was a quick, dainty little thing with dark gold hair that went a soft brown, and wide, slightly prominent blue eyes that were at once so candid and so knowing. She was always grown up; she never really grew up. Always strangely wise, and always childish.

It was her father's fault.

"My little Princess must never take too much notice of people and the things they say and do," he repeated to her. "People don't know what they are doing and saying. They chatter-chatter, and they hurt one another, and they hurt themselves very often, till they cry. But don't take any notice, my little Princess. Because it is all nothing. Inside everybody there is another creature, a demon which doesn't care at all. You peel away all the things they say and do and feel, as cook peels away the outside of the onions. And in the middle of everybody there is a green demon which you can't peel away. And this green demon never changes, and it doesn't care at all about all the things that happen to the outside leaves of the person, all the chatter-chatter, and all the husbands and wives and children, and troubles and fusses. You peel everything away from people, and there is a green, upright demon in every man and woman; and this demon is a man's real self, and a woman's real self. It doesn't really care about anybody, it belongs to the demons and the primitive fairies, who never care. But, even so, there are big demons and mean demons, and splendid demonish fairies, and vulgar ones. But there are no royal fairy women left. Only you, my little Princess. You are the last of the royal race of the old people; the last, my Princess. There are no others. You and I are the last. When I am dead there will be only you. And that is why, darling, you will never care for any of the people in the world very much. Because their demons are all dwindled and vulgar. They are not royal. Only you are royal, after me. Always remember that. And always remember, it is a *great secret.* If you tell people, they will try to kill you, because they will envy you for being a Princess. It is our great secret, darling. I am a prince, and you a princess, of the old, old blood. And we keep our secret between us, all alone. And so, darling, you must treat all people very politely, because *noblesse oblige.* But you must never forget that you alone are the last of Princesses, and that all other are less than you are, less noble, more vulgar. Treat them politely and gently and kindly, darling. But you are the Princess, and they are commoners. Never try to think of them as if they were like you. They are not. You will find, always, that they are lacking, lacking in the royal touch, which only you have—"

The Princess learned her lesson early – the first lesson, of absolute reticence, the impossibility of intimacy with any other than her father; the second lesson, of naïve, slightly benevolent politeness. As a small child, something crystallised in her character, making her clear and finished, and as impervious as crystal.

"Dear child!" her hostesses said of her. "She is so quaint and old-fashioned; such a lady, poor little mite!"

She was erect, and very dainty. Always small, nearly tiny in physique, she seemed like a changeling beside her big, handsome, slightly mad father. She dressed very simply, usually in blue or delicate greys, with little collars of old Milan point, or very finely-worked linen. She had exquisite little hands, that made the piano sound like a spinet when she played. She was rather given to wearing cloaks and capes, instead of coats, out of doors, and little eighteenth-century sort of hats. Her complexion was pure apple-blossom.

She looked as if she had stepped out of a picture. But no one, to her dying day, ever knew exactly the strange picture her father had framed her in and from which she never stepped.

Her grandfather and grandmother and her Aunt Maud demanded twice to see her, once in Rome and once in Paris. Each time they were charmed, piqued, and annoyed. She was so exquisite and such a little virgin. At the same time so knowing and so oddly assured. That odd, assured touch of condescension, and the inward coldness, infuriated her American relations.

Only she really fascinated her grandfather. He was spellbound; in a way, in love with the little faultless thing. His wife would catch him brooding, musing over his grandchild, long months after the meeting, and craving to see her again. He cherished to the end the fond hope that she might come to live with him and her grandmother.

"Thank you so much, grandfather. You are so very kind. But Papa and I are such an old couple, you see, such a crochety old couple, living in a world of our own."

Her father let her see the world – from the outside. And he let her read. When she was in her teens she read Zola and Maupassant, and with the eyes of Zola and Maupassant she looked on Paris. A little later she read Tolstoi and Dostoevsky. The latter confused her. The others, she seemed to understand with a very shrewd, canny understanding, just as she understood the Decameron stories as she read them in their old Italian, or the Nibelung poems. Strange and *uncanny,* she seemed to understand things in a cold light perfectly, with all the flush of fire absent. She was something like a changeling, not quite human.

This earned her, also, strange antipathies. Cabmen and railway porters, especially in Paris and Rome, would suddenly treat her with brutal rudeness, when she was alone. They seemed to look on her with sudden violent antipathy. They sensed in her curious impertinence, an easy, sterile impertinence towards the things *they* felt most. She was so assured, and her flower of maidenhood was so scentless. She could look at a lusty, sensual Roman cabman as if he were a sort of grotesque, to make her smile. She knew all about him, in Zola. And the peculiar condescension with which she would give him her order, as if she, frail, beautiful thing, were the only reality, and he, coarse monster, was a sort of Caliban floundering in the mud on the margin of the pool of the perfect lotus, would suddenly enrage the fellow, the real Mediterranean who prided himself on his *beauté male,* and to whom the phallic mystery was still the only mystery. And he would turn a terrible face on her, bully her in a brutal, coarse fashion – hideous. For to him she had only the blasphemous impertinence of her own sterility.

Encounters like these made her tremble, and made her know she must have support from the outside. The power of her spirit did not extend to these low people, and they had all the physical power. She realised an implacability of hatred in their turning on her. But she did not lose her head. She quietly paid out money and turned away.

Those were dangerous moments, though, and she learned to be prepared for them. The Princess she was, and the fairy from the North, and could never understand the volcanic phallic rage with which coarse people could turn on her in a paroxysm of hatred. They never turned on her father like that. And quite early she decided it was the New England mother in her whom they hated. Never for one minute could she see with the old Roman eyes, see herself as sterility, the barren flower taking on airs and an intolerable impertinence. This was what the Roman cabman saw in her. And he longed to crush the barren blossom. Its sexless beauty and its authority put him in a passion of brutal revolt.

When she was nineteen her grandfather died, leaving her a considerable fortune in the safe hands of responsible trustees. They would deliver her her income, but only on condition that she resided for six months in the year in the United States.

"Why should they make me conditions?" she said to her father. "I refuse to be imprisoned six months in the year in the United States. We will tell them to keep their money."

"Let us be wise, my little Princess, let us be wise. No, we are almost poor, and we are never safe from rudeness. I cannot allow anybody to be rude to me. I hate it, I hate it!" His eyes flamed as he said it. "I could kill any man or woman who is rude to me. But we are in exile in the world. We are powerless. If we were really poor, we should be quite powerless, and then I should die. No, my Princess. Let us take their money, then they will not dare to be rude to us. Let us take it, as we put on clothes, to cover ourselves from their aggressions."

There began a new phase, when the father and daughter spent their summers on the Great Lakes or in California, or in the South-West. The father was something of a poet, the daughter something of a painter. He wrote poems about the lakes or the redwood trees, and she made dainty drawings. He was physically a strong man, and he loved the out-of-doors. He would go off with her for days, paddling in a canoe and sleeping by a camp-fire. Frail little Princess, she was always undaunted, always undaunted. She would ride with him on horseback over the mountain trails till she was so tired she was nothing but a bodiless consciousness sitting astride her pony. But she never gave in. And at night he folded her in her blanket on a bed of balsam pine twigs, and she lay and looked at the stars unmurmuring. She was fulfilling her role.

People said to her as the years passed, and she was a woman of twenty-five, then a woman of thirty, and always the same virgin dainty Princess, 'knowing' in a dispassionate way, like an old woman, and utterly intact:

"Don't you ever think what you will do when your father is no longer with you?"

She looked at her interlocutor with that cold, elfin detachment of hers:

"No, I never think of it," she said.

She had a tiny, but exquisite little house in London, and another small, perfect house in Connecticut, each with a faithful housekeeper. Two homes, if she chose. And she knew many interesting literary and artistic people. What more?

So the years passed imperceptibly. And she had that quality of the sexless fairies, she did not change. At thirty-three she looked twenty-three.

Her father, however, was ageing, and becoming more and more queer. It was now her task to be his guardian in his private madness. He spent the last three years of life in the house in Connecticut. He was very much estranged, sometimes had fits of violence which almost killed the little Princess. Physical violence was horrible to her; it seemed to shatter her heart. But she found a woman a few years younger than herself, well-educated and sensitive, to be a sort of nurse-companion to the mad old man. So the fact of madness was never openly admitted. Miss Cummins, the companion, had a passionate loyalty to the Princess, and a curious affection, tinged with love, for the handsome, white-haired, courteous old man, who was never at all aware of his fits of violence once they had passed.

The Princess was thirty-eight years old when her father died. And quite unchanged. She was still tiny, and like a dignified, scentless flower. Her soft brownish hair, almost the colour of beaver fur, was bobbed, and fluffed softly round her apple-blossom face, that was modelled with an arched nose like a proud old Florentine portrait. In her voice, manner and bearing she was exceedingly still, like a flower that has blossomed in a shadowy place. And from her blue eyes looked out the Princess's eternal laconic challenge, that grew almost sardonic as the years passed. She was the Princess, and sardonically she looked out on a princeless world.

She was relieved when her father died, and at the same time, it was as if everything had evaporated around her. She had lived in a sort of hot-house, in the aura of her father's madness. Suddenly the hot-house had been removed from around her, and she was in the raw, vast, vulgar open air.

Quoi faire? What was she to do? She seemed faced with absolute nothingness. Only she had Miss Cummins, who shared with her the secret, and almost the passion for her father. In fact, the Princess felt that her passion for her mad father had in some curious way transferred itself largely to Charlotte Cummins during the last years. And now Miss Cummins was the vessel that held the passion for the dead man. She herself, the Princess, was an empty vessel.

An empty vessel in the enormous warehouse of the world.

Quoi faire? What was she to do? She felt that, since she could not evaporate into nothingness, like alcohol from an unstoppered bottle, she must *do* something. Never before in her life had she felt the incumbency. Never, never had she felt she must *do* anything. That was left to the vulgar.

Now her father was dead, she found herself on the *fringe* of the vulgar crowd, sharing their necessity to *do* something. It was a little humiliating. She felt herself becoming vulgarised. At the same time she found herself looking at men with a shrewder eye: an eye to marriage. Not that she felt any sudden interest in men, or attraction towards them. No. She was still neither interested nor attracted towards men vitally. But *marriage*, that peculiar abstraction, had imposed a sort of spell on her. She thought that *marriage*, in the blank abstract, was the thing she ought to *do*. That *marriage* implied a man she also knew. She knew all the facts. But the man seemed a property of her own mind rather than a thing in himself, another thing.

Her father died in the summer, the month after her thirty-eighth birthday. When all was over, the obvious thing to do, of course, was to travel. With Miss Cummins. The two women knew each other intimately, but they were always Miss Urquhart and Miss Cummins to one another, and a certain distance was instinctively maintained. Miss Cummins, from Philadelphia, of scholastic stock, and intelligent but untravelled, four years younger than the Princess, felt herself immensely the junior of her 'lady'. She had a sort of passionate veneration for the Princess, who seemed to her ageless, timeless. She could not see the rows of tiny, dainty, exquisite shoes in the Princess's cupboard without feeling a stab at the heart, a stab of tenderness and reverence, almost of awe.

Miss Cummins also was virginal, but with a look of puzzled surprise in her brown eyes. Her skin was pale and clear, her features well modelled, but there was a certain blankness in her expression, where the Princess had an odd touch of Renaissance grandeur. Miss Cummins's voice was also hushed almost to a whisper; it was the inevitable effect of Colin Urquhart's room. But the hushedness had a hoarse quality.

The Princess did not want to go to Europe. Her face seemed turned west. Now her father was gone, she felt she would go west, westwards, as if forever. Following, no doubt, the March of Empire, which is brought up rather short on the Pacific coast, among swarms of wallowing bathers.

No, not the Pacific coast. She would stop short of that. The South-West was less vulgar. She would go to New Mexico.

She and Miss Cummins arrived at the Rancho del Cerro Gordo towards the end of August, when the crowd was beginning to drift back east. The ranch lay by a stream on the desert some four miles from the foot of the mountains, a mile away from the Indian pueblo of San Cristobal. It was a ranch for the rich; the Princess paid thirty dollars a day for herself and Miss Cummins. But then she had a little cottage to herself, among the apple trees of the orchard, with an excellent cook. She and Miss Cummins, however, took dinner at evening in the large guesthouse. For the Princess still entertained the idea of *marriage*.

The guests at the Rancho del Cerro Gordo were of all sorts, except the poor sort. They were practically all rich, and many were romantic. Some were charming, others were vulgar, some were movie people, quite quaint and not unattractive in their vulgarity, and many were Jews. The Princess did not care for Jews, though they were usually the most interesting to *talk* to. So she talked a good deal with the Jews, and painted with the artists, and rode with the young men from college, and had altogether quite a good time. And yet she felt something of a fish out of water, or a bird in the wrong forest. And *marriage* remained still completely in the abstract. No connecting it with any of these young men, even the nice ones.

The Princess looked just twenty-five. The freshness of her mouth, the hushed, delicate-complexioned virginity of her face gave her not a day more. Only a certain laconic look in her eyes was disconcerting. When she was *forced* to write her age, she put twenty-eight, making the figure *two* rather badly, so that it just avoided being a three.

Men hinted marriage at her. Especially boys from college suggested it from a distance. But they all failed before the look of sardonic ridicule in the Princess's eyes. It always seemed to her rather preposterous, quite ridiculous, and a tiny bit impertinent on their part.

The only man that intrigued her at all was one of the guides, a man called Romero – Domingo Romero. It was he who had sold the ranch itself to the Wilkiesons, ten years before, for two thousand dollars. He had gone away, then reappeared at the old place. For he was the son of the old Romero, the last of the Spanish family that had owned miles of land around San Cristobal. But the coming of the white man and the failure of the vast flocks of sheep, and the fatal inertia which overcomes all men, at last, on the desert near the mountains, had finished the Romero family. The last descendants were just Mexican peasants.

Domingo, the heir, had spent his two thousand dollars, and was working for white people. He was now about thirty years old, a tall, silent fellow, with a heavy closed mouth and black eyes that looked across at one almost sullenly. From behind he was handsome, with a strong, natural body, and the back of his neck very dark and well-shapen, strong with life. But his dark face was long and heavy, almost sinister, with that peculiar heavy meaninglessness in it, characteristic of the Mexicans of his own locality. They are strong, they seem healthy. They laugh and joke with one another. But their physique and their natures seem static, as if there were nowhere, nowhere at all for their energies to go, and their faces, degenerating to misshapen heaviness, seem to have no *raison d'être,* no radical meaning. Waiting either to die or to be aroused into passion and hope. In some of the black eyes a queer, haunting mystic quality, sombre and a bit gruesome, the skull-and-cross-bones look of the Penitentes. They had found their *raison d'être* in self-torture and death-worship. Unable to wrest a *positive* significance for themselves from the vast, beautiful, but vindictive landscape they were born into, they turned on their own selves, and worshipped death through self-torture. The mystic gloom of this showed in their eyes.

But as a rule the dark eyes of the Mexicans were heavy and half alive, sometimes hostile, sometimes kindly, often with the fatal Indian glaze on them, or the fatal Indian glint.

Domingo Romero was *almost* a typical Mexican to look at, with the typical heavy, dark, long face, clean-shaven, with an almost brutally heavy mouth. His eyes were black and Indian-looking. Only, at the centre of their hopelessness was a spark of pride, or self-confidence, or dauntlessness. Just a spark in the midst of the blackness of static despair.

But this spark was the difference between him and the mass of men. It gave a certain alert sensitiveness to his bearing and a certain beauty to his appearance. He wore a low-crowned black hat, instead of the ponderous headgear of the usual Mexican, and his clothes were thinnish and graceful. Silent, aloof, almost imperceptible in the landscape, he was an admirable guide, with a startling quick intelligence that anticipated difficulties about to rise. He could cook, too, crouching over the camp-fire and moving his lean deft brown hands. The only fault he had was that he was not forthcoming, he wasn't chatty and cosy.

"Oh, don't send Romero with us," the Jews would say. "One can't get any response from him."

Tourists come and go, but they rarely *see* anything, inwardly. None of them ever saw the spark at the middle of Romero's eye; they were not alive enough to see it.

The Princess caught it one day, when she had him for a guide. She was fishing for trout in the canyon, Miss Cummins was reading a book, the horses were tied under the trees, Romero was fixing a proper fly on her line. He fixed the fly and handed her the line, looking up at her. And at that moment she caught the spark in his eye. And instantly she knew that he was a gentleman, that his 'demon', as her father would have said, was a fine demon. And instantly her manner towards him changed.

He had perched her on a rock over a quiet pool, beyond the cotton-wood trees. It was early September, and the canyon already cool, but the leaves of the cottonwoods were still green. The Princess stood on her rock, a small but perfectly-formed figure, wearing a soft, close grey sweater and neatly-cut grey riding-breeches, with tall black boots, her fluffy brown hair straggling from under a little grey felt hat. A woman? Not quite. A changeling of some sort, perched in outline there on the rock, in the bristling wild canyon. She knew perfectly well how to handle a line. Her father had made a fisherman of her.

Romero, in a black shirt and with loose black trousers pushed into wide black riding-boots, was fishing a little farther down.

He had put his hat on a rock behind him; his dark head was bent a little forward, watching the water. He had caught three trout. From time to time he glanced up-stream at the Princess, perched there so daintily. He saw she had caught nothing.

Soon he quietly drew in his line and came up to her. His keen eye watched her line, watched her position. Then, quietly, he suggested certain changes to her, putting his sensitive brown hand before her. And he withdrew a little, and stood in silence, leaning against a tree, watching her. He was helping her across the distance. She knew it, and thrilled. And in a moment she had a bite. In two minutes she landed a good trout. She looked round at him quickly, her eyes sparkling, the colour heightened in her cheeks. And as she met his eyes a smile of greeting went over his dark face, very sudden, with an odd sweetness.

She knew he was helping her. And she felt in his presence a subtle, insidious male *kindliness* she had never known before waiting upon her. Her cheek flushed, and her blue eyes darkened.

After this, she always looked for him, and for that curious dark beam of a man's kindliness which he could give her, as it were, from his chest, from his heart. It was something she had never known before.

A vague, unspoken intimacy grew up between them. She liked his voice, his appearance, his presence. His natural language was Spanish; he spoke English like a foreign language, rather slow, with a slight hesitation, but with a sad, plangent sonority lingering over from his Spanish. There was a certain subtle correctness in his appearance; he was always perfectly shaved; his hair was thick and rather long on top, but always carefully groomed behind. And his fine black cashmere shirt, his wide leather belt, his well-cut, wide black trousers going into the embroidered cowboy boots had a certain inextinguishable elegance. He wore no silver rings or buckles. Only his boots were embroidered and decorated at the top with an inlay of white *suède.* He seemed elegant, slender, yet he was very strong.

And at the same time, curiously, he gave her the feeling that death was not far from him. Perhaps he too was half in love with death. However that may be, the sense she had that death was not far from him made him 'possible' to her.

Small as she was, she was quite a good horsewoman. They gave her at the ranch a sorrel mare, very lovely in colour, and well-made, with a powerful broad neck and the hollow back that betokens a swift runner. Tansy, she was called. Her only fault was the usual mare's failing, she was inclined to be hysterical.

So that every day the Princess set off with Miss Cummins and Romero, on horseback, riding into the mountains. Once they went camping for several days, with two more friends in the party.

"I think I like it better," the Princess said to Romero, "when we three go alone."

And he gave her one of his quick, transfiguring smiles.

It was curious no white man had ever showed her this capacity for subtle gentleness, this power to *help* her in silence across a distance, if she were fishing without success, or tired of her horse, or if Tansy suddenly got scared. It was as if Romero could send her *from his heart* a dark beam of succour and sustaining. She had never known this before, and it was very thrilling.

Then the smile that suddenly creased his dark face, showing the strong white teeth. It creased his face almost into a savage grotesque. And at the same time there was in it something so warm, such a dark flame of kindliness for her, she was elated into her true Princess self.

Then that vivid, latent spark in his eye, which she had seen, and which she knew he was aware she had seen. It made an inter-recognition between them, silent and delicate. Here he was delicate as a woman in this subtle inter-recognition.

And yet his presence only put to flight in her the *idée fixe* of 'marriage'. For some reason, in her strange little brain, the idea of *marrying* him could not enter. Not for any definite reason. He was in himself a gentleman, and she had plenty of money for two. There was no actual obstacle. Nor was she conventional.

No, now she came down to it, it was as if their two 'dæmons' could marry, were perhaps married. Only their two *selves*, Miss Urquhart and Señor Domingo Romero, were for some reason incompatible. There was a peculiar subtle intimacy of inter-recognition between them. But she did not see in the least how it would lead to marriage. Almost she could more easily marry one of the nice boys from Harvard or Yale.

The time passed, and she let it pass. The end of September came, with aspens going yellow on the mountain heights, and oak-scrub going red. But as yet the cottonwoods in the valley and canyons had not changed.

"When will you go away?" Romero asked her, looking at her fixedly, with a blank black eye.

"By the end of October," she said. "I have promised to be in Santa Barbara at the beginning of November."

He was hiding the spark in his eye from her. But she saw the peculiar sullen thickening of his heavy mouth.

She had complained to him many times that one never saw any wild animals, except chipmunks and squirrels, and perhaps a skunk and a porcupine. Never a deer, or a bear, or a mountain lion.

"Are there no bigger animals in these mountains?" she asked, dissatisfied.

"Yes," he said. "There are deer – I see their tracks. And I saw the tracks of a bear."

"But why can one never see the animals themselves?" She looked dissatisfied and wistful like a child.

"Why, it's pretty hard for you to see them. They won't let you come close. You have to keep still, in a place where they come. Or else you have to follow their tracks a long way."

"I can't bear to go away till I've seen them: a bear, or a deer—"

The smile came suddenly on his face, indulgent.

"Well, what do you want? Do you want to go up into the mountains to some place, to wait till they come?"

"Yes," she said, looking up at him with a sudden naïve impulse of recklessness.

And immediately his face became sombre again, responsible.

"Well," he said, with slight irony, a touch of mockery of her. "You will have to find a house. It's very cold at night now. You would have to stay all night in a house."

"And there are no houses up there?" she said.

"Yes," he replied. "There is a little shack that belongs to me, that a miner built a long time ago, looking for gold. You can go there and stay one night, and maybe you see something. Maybe! I don't know. Maybe nothing come."

"How much chance is there?"

"Well, I don't know. Last time when I was there I see three deer come down to drink at the water, and I shot two raccoons. But maybe this time we don't see anything."

"Is there water there?" she asked.

"Yes, there is a little round pond, you know, below the spruce trees. And the water from the snow runs into it."

"Is it far away?" she asked.

"Yes, pretty far. You see that ridge there" – and turning to the mountains he lifted his arm in the gesture which is somehow so moving, out in the West, pointing to the distance – "that ridge where there are no trees, only rock" – his black eyes were focussed on the distance, his face impassive, but as if in pain – "you go round that ridge, and along, then you come down through the spruce trees to where that cabin is. My father bought that placer claim from a miner who was broke, but nobody ever found any gold or anything, and nobody ever goes there. Too lonesome!"

The Princess watched the massive, heavy-sitting, beautiful bulk of the Rocky Mountains. It was early in October, and the aspens were already losing their gold leaves; high up, the spruce and pine seemed to be growing darker; the great flat patches of oak scrub on the heights were red like gore.

"Can I go over there?" she asked, turning to him and meeting the spark in his eye.

His face was heavy with responsibility.

"Yes," he said, "you can go. But there'll be snow over the ridge, and it's awful cold, and awful lonesome."

"I should like to go," she said, persistent.

"All right," he said. "You can go if you want to."

She doubted, though, if the Wilkiesons would let her go; at least alone with Romero and Miss Cummins.

Yet an obstinacy characteristic of her nature, an obstinacy tinged perhaps with madness, had taken hold of her. She wanted to look over the mountains into their secret heart. She wanted to descend to the cabin below the spruce trees, near the tarn of bright green water. She wanted to see the wild animals move about in their wild unconsciousness.

"Let us say to the Wilkiesons that we want to make the trip round the Frijoles canyon," she said.

The trip round the Frijoles canyon was a usual thing. It would not be strenuous, nor cold, nor lonely: they could sleep in the log house that was called an hotel.

Romero looked at her quickly.

"If you want to say that," he replied, "you can tell Mrs. Wilkieson. Only I know she'll be mad with me if I take you up in the mountains to that place. And I've got to go there first with a pack-horse, to take lots of blankets and some bread. Maybe Miss Cummins can't stand it. Maybe not. It's a hard trip."

He was speaking, and thinking, in the heavy, disconnected Mexican fashion.

"Never mind!" The Princess was suddenly very decisive and stiff with authority. "I want to do it. I will arrange with Mrs. Wilkieson. And we'll go on Saturday."

He shook his head slowly.

"I've got to go up on Sunday with a pack-horse and blankets," he said. "Can't do it before."

"Very well!" she said, rather piqued. "Then we'll start on Monday."

She hated being thwarted even the tiniest bit.

He knew that if he started with the pack on Sunday at dawn he would not be back until late at night. But he consented that they should start on Monday morning at seven. The obedient Miss Cummins was told to prepare for the Frijoles trip. On Sunday Romero had his day off. He had not put in an appearance when the Princess retired on Sunday night, but on Monday morning, as she was dressing, she saw him bringing in the three horses from the corral. She was in high spirits.

The night had been cold. There was ice at the edges of the irrigation ditch, and the chipmunks crawled into the sun and lay with wide, dumb, anxious eyes, almost too numb to run.

"We may be away two or three days," said the Princess.

"Very well. We won't begin to be anxious about you before Thursday, then," said Mrs. Wilkieson, who was young and capable: from Chicago. "Anyway," she added, "Romero will see you through. He's so trustworthy."

The sun was already on the desert as they set off towards the mountains, making the greasewood and the sage pale as pale-grey sands, luminous the great level around them. To the right glinted the shadows of the adobe pueblo, flat and almost invisible on the plain, earth of its earth. Behind lay the ranch and the tufts of tall, plumy cottonwoods, whose summits were yellowing under the perfect blue sky.

Autumn breaking into colour in the great spaces of the South-West.

But the three trotted gently along the trail, towards the sun that sparkled yellow just above the dark bulk of the ponderous mountains. Side-slopes were already gleaming yellow, flaming with a second light, under coldish blue of the pale sky. The front slopes were in shadow, with submerged lustre of red oak scrub and dull-gold aspens, blue-black pines and grey-blue rock. While the canyon was full of a deep blueness.

They rode single file, Romero first, on a black horse. Himself in black, made a flickering black spot in the delicate pallor of the great landscape, where even pine trees at a distance take a film of blue paler than their green. Romero rode on in silence past the tufts of furry greasewood. The Princess came next, on her sorrel mare. And Miss Cummins, who was not quite happy on horseback, came last, in the pale dust that the others kicked up. Sometimes her horse sneezed, and she started.

But on they went at a gentle trot. Romero never looked round. He could hear the sound of the hoofs following, and that was all he wanted.

For the rest, he held ahead. And the Princess, with that black, unheeding figure always travelling away from her, felt strangely helpless, withal elated.

They neared the pale, round foot-hills, dotted with the round dark piñon and cedar shrubs. The horses clinked and trotted among the stones. Occasionally a big round greasewood held out fleecy tufts of flowers, pure gold. They wound into blue shadow, then up a steep stony slope, with the world lying pallid away behind and below. Then they dropped into the shadow of the San Cristobal canyon.

The stream was running full and swift. Occasionally the horses snatched at a tuft of grass. The trail narrowed and became rocky; the rocks closed in; it was dark and cool as the horses climbed and climbed upwards, and the tree trunks crowded in the shadowy, silent tightness of the canyon. They were among cottonwood trees that ran straight up and smooth and round to an extraordinary height. Above, the tips were gold, and it was sun. But away below, where the horses struggled up the rocks and wound among the trunks, there was still blue shadow by the sound of waters and an occasional grey festoon of old man's beard, and here and there a pale, dripping crane's-bill flower among the tangle and the débris of the virgin place. And again the chill entered the Princess's heart as she realised what a tangle of decay and despair lay in the virgin forests.

They scrambled downwards, splashed across stream, up rocks and along the trail of the other side. Romero's black horse stopped, looked down quizzically at the fallen trees, then stepped over lightly. The Princess's sorrel followed, carefully. But Miss Cummins's buckskin made a fuss, and had to be got round.

In the same silence, save for the clinking of the horses and the splashing as the trail crossed stream, they worked their way upwards in the tight, tangled shadow of the canyon. Sometimes, crossing stream, the Princess would glance upwards, and then always her heart caught in her breast. For high up, away in heaven, the mountain heights shone yellow, dappled with dark spruce firs, clear almost as speckled daffodils against the pale turquoise blue lying high and serene above the dark-blue shadow where the Princess was. And she would snatch at the blood-red leaves of the oak as her horse crossed a more open slope, not knowing what she felt.

They were getting fairly high, occasionally lifted above the canyon itself, in the low groove below the speckled, gold-sparkling heights which towered beyond. Then again they dipped and crossed stream, the horses stepping gingerly across a tangle of fallen, frail aspen stems, then suddenly floundering in a mass of rocks. The black emerged ahead, his black tail waving. The Princess let her mare find her own footing; then she too emerged from the clatter. She rode on after the black. Then came a great frantic rattle of the buckskin behind. The Princess was aware of Romero's dark face looking round, with a strange, demon-like watchfulness, before she herself looked round, to see the buckskin scrambling rather lamely beyond the rocks, with one of his pale buff knees already red with blood.

"He almost went down!" called Miss Cummins.

But Romero was already out of the saddle and hastening down the path. He made quiet little noises to the buckskin, and began examining the cut knee.

"Is he hurt?" cried Miss Cummins anxiously, and she climbed hastily down.

"Oh, my goodness!" she cried, as she saw the blood running down the slender buff leg of the horse in a thin trickle. "Isn't that *awful?*" She spoke in a stricken voice, and her face was white.

Romero was still carefully feeling the knee of the buckskin. Then he made him walk a few paces. And at last he stood up straight and shook his head.

"Not very bad!" he said. "Nothing broken."

Again he bent and worked at the knees. Then he looked up at the Princess.

"He can go on," he said. "It's not bad."

The Princess looked down at the dark face in silence.

"What, go on right up here?" cried Miss Cummins. "How many hours?"

"About five!" said Romero simply.

"Five hours!" cried Miss Cummins. "A horse with a lame knee! And a steep mountain! Why-y!"

"Yes, it's pretty steep up there," said Romero, pushing back his hat and staring fixedly at the bleeding knee. The buckskin stood in a stricken sort of dejection. "But I think he'll make it all right," the man added.

"Oh!" cried Miss Cummins, her eyes bright with sudden passion of unshed tears. "I wouldn't think of it. I wouldn't ride him up there, not for any money."

"Why wouldn't you?" asked Romero.

"It *hurts* him."

Romero bent down again to the horse's knee.

"Maybe it hurts him a little," he said. "But he can make it all right, and his leg won't get stiff."

"What! Ride him five hours up the steep mountains?" cried Miss Cummins. "I couldn't. I just couldn't do it. I'll lead him a little way and see if he can go. But I *couldn't* ride him again. I couldn't. Let me walk."

"But Miss Cummins, dear, if Romero says he'll be all right?" said the Princess.

"I know it hurts him. Oh, I just couldn't bear it."

There was no doing anything with Miss Cummins. The thought of a hurt animal always put her into a sort of hysterics.

They walked forward a little, leading the buckskin. He limped rather badly. Miss Cummins sat on a rock.

"Why, it's agony to see him!" she cried. "It's *cruel!*"

"He won't limp after a bit, if you take no notice of him," said Romero. "Now he plays up, and limps very much, because he wants to make you see."

"I don't think there can be much playing up," said Miss Cummins bitterly. "We can see how it must hurt him."

"It don't hurt much," said Romero.

But now Miss Cummins was silent with antipathy.

It was a deadlock. The party remained motionless on the trail, the Princess in the saddle, Miss Cummins seated on a rock, Romero standing black and remote near the drooping buckskin.

"Well!" said the man suddenly at last. "I guess we go back, then."

And he looked up swiftly at his horse, which was cropping at the mountain herbage and treading on the trailing reins.

"No!" cried the Princess. "Oh no!" Her voice rang with a great wail of disappointment and anger. Then she checked herself.

Miss Cummins rose with energy.

"Let me lead the buckskin home," she said, with cold dignity, "and you two go on."

This was received in silence. The Princess was looking down at her with a sardonic, almost cruel gaze.

"We've only come about two hours," said Miss Cummins. "I don't mind a bit leading him home. But I *couldn't* ride him. I *couldn't* have him ridden with that knee."

This again was received in dead silence. Romero remained impassive, almost inert.

"Very well, then," said the Princess. "You lead him home. You'll be quite all right. Nothing can happen to you, possibly. And say to them that we have gone on and shall be home tomorrow – or the day after."

She spoke coldly and distinctly. For she could not bear to be thwarted.

"Better all go back, and come again another day," said Romero – non-committal.

"There will never *be* another day," cried the Princess. "I want to go on."

She looked at him square in the eyes, and met the spark in his eye.

He raised his shoulders slightly.

"If you want it," he said. "I'll go on with you. But Miss Cummins can ride my horse to the end of the canyon, and I lead the buckskin. Then I come back to you."

It was arranged so. Miss Cummins had her saddle put on Romero's black horse, Romero took the buckskin's bridle, and they started back. The Princess rode very slowly on, upwards, alone. She was at first so angry with Miss Cummins that she was blind to everything else. She just let her mare follow her own inclinations.

The peculiar spell of anger carried the Princess on, almost unconscious, for an hour or so. And by this time she was beginning to climb pretty high. Her horse walked steadily all the time. They emerged on a bare slope, and the trail wound through frail aspen stems. Here a wind swept, and some of the aspens were already bare. Others were fluttering their discs of pure, solid yellow leaves, so *nearly* like petals, while the slope ahead was one soft, glowing fleece of daffodil yellow; fleecy like a golden foxskin, and yellow as daffodils alive in the wind and the high mountain sun.

She paused and looked back. The near great slopes were mottled with gold and the dark hue of spruce, like some unsinged eagle, and the light lay gleaming upon them. Away through the gap of the canyon she could see the pale blue of the egg-like desert, with the crumpled dark crack of the Rio Grande Canyon. And far, far off, the blue mountains like a fence of angels on the horizon.

And she thought of her adventure. She was going on alone with Romero. But then she was very sure of herself, and Romero was not the kind of man to do anything to her against her will. This was her first thought. And she just had a fixed desire to go over the brim of the mountains, to look into the inner chaos of the Rockies. And she wanted to go with Romero, because he had some peculiar kinship with her; there was some peculiar link between the two of them. Miss Cummins anyhow would have been only a discordant note.

She rode on, and emerged at length in the lap of the summit. Beyond her was a great concave of stone and stark, dead-grey trees, where the mountain ended against the sky. But nearer was the dense black, bristling spruce, and at her feet was the lap of the summit, a flat little valley of sere grass and quiet-standing yellow aspens, the stream trickling like a thread across.

It was a little valley or shell from which the stream was gently poured into the lower rocks and trees of the canyon. Around her was a fairy-like gentleness, the delicate sere grass, the groves of delicate-stemmed aspens dropping their flakes of bright yellow. And the delicate, quick little stream threading through the wild, sere grass.

Here one might expect deer and fawns and wild things, as in a little paradise. Here she was to wait for Romero, and they were to have lunch.

She unfastened her saddle and pulled it to the ground with a crash, letting her horse wander with a long rope. How beautiful Tansy looked, sorrel, among the yellow leaves that lay like a patina on the sere ground. The Princess herself wore a fleecy sweater of a pale, sere buff, like the grass, and riding-breeches of a pure orange-tawny colour. She felt quite in the picture.

From her saddle-pouches she took the packages of lunch, spread a little cloth, and sat to wait for Romero. Then she made a little fire. Then she ate a devilled egg. Then she ran after Tansy, who was straying across-stream. Then she sat in the sun, in the stillness near the aspens, and waited.

The sky was blue. Her little alp was soft and delicate as fairyland. But beyond and up jutted the great slopes, dark with the pointed feathers of spruce, bristling with grey dead trees among grey rock, or dappled with dark and gold. The beautiful, but fierce, heavy cruel mountains, with their moments of tenderness.

She saw Tansy start, and begin to run. Two ghost-like figures on horseback emerged from the black of the spruce across the stream. It was two Indians on horseback, swathed like seated mummies in their pale-grey cotton blankets. Their guns jutted beyond the saddles. They rode straight towards her, to her thread of smoke.

As they came near, they unswathed themselves and greeted her, looking at her curiously from their dark eyes. Their black hair was somewhat untidy, the long rolled plaits on their shoulders were soiled. They looked tired.

They got down from their horses near her little fire – a camp was a camp – swathed their blankets round their hips, pulled the saddles from their ponies and turned them loose, then sat down. One was a young Indian whom she had met before, the other was an older man.

"You all alone?" said the younger man.

"Romero will be here in a minute," she said, glancing back along the trail.

"Ah, Romero! You with him? Where are you going?"

"Round the ridge," she said. "Where are you going?"

"We going down to Pueblo."

"Been out hunting? How long have you been out?"

"Yes. Been out five days." The young Indian gave a little meaningless laugh.

"Got anything?"

"No. We see tracks of two deer – but not got nothing."

The Princess noticed a suspicious-looking bulk under one of the saddles – surely a folded-up deer. But she said nothing.

"You must have been cold," she said.

"Yes, very cold in the night. And hungry. Got nothing to eat since yesterday. Eat it all up." And again he laughed his little meaningless laugh. Under their dark skins, the two men looked peaked and hungry. The Princess rummaged for food among the saddle-bags. There was a lump of bacon – the regular stand-back – and some bread. She gave them this, and they began toasting slices of it on long sticks at the fire. Such was the little camp Romero saw as he rode down the slope: the Princess in her orange breeches, her head tied in a blue-and-brown silk kerchief, sitting opposite the two dark-headed Indians across the camp-fire, while one of the Indians was leaning forward toasting bacon, his two plaits of braid-hair dangling as if wearily.

Romero rode up, his face expressionless. The Indians greeted him in Spanish. He unsaddled his horse, took food from the bags, and sat down at the camp to eat. The Princess went to the stream for water, and to wash her hands.

"Got coffee?" asked the Indians.

"No coffee this outfit," said Romero.

They lingered an hour or more in the warm midday sun. Then Romero saddled the horses. The Indians still squatted by the fire. Romero and the Princess rode away, calling *Adios!* to the Indians over the stream and into the dense spruce whence two strange figures had emerged.

When they were alone, Romero turned and looked at her curiously, in a way she could not understand, with such a hard glint in his eyes. And for the first time she wondered if she was rash.

"I hope you don't mind going alone with me," she said.

"If you want it," he replied.

They emerged at the foot of the great bare slope of rocky summit, where dead spruce trees stood sparse and bristling like bristles on a grey dead hog. Romero said the Mexicans, twenty years back, had fired the mountains, to drive out the whites. This grey concave slope of summit was corpse-like.

The trail was almost invisible. Romero watched for the trees which the Forest Service had blazed. And they climbed the stark corpse slope, among dead spruce, fallen and ash-grey, into the wind. The wind came rushing from the west, up the funnel of the canyon, from the desert. And there was the desert, like a vast mirage tilting slowly upwards towards the west, immense and pallid, away beyond the funnel of the canyon. The Princess could hardly look.

For an hour their horses rushed the slope, hastening with a great working of the haunches upwards, and halting to breathe, scrambling again, and rowing their way up length by length, on the livid, slanting wall. While the wind blew like some vast machine.

After an hour they were working their way on the incline, no longer forcing straight up. All was grey and dead around them; the horses picked their way over the silver-grey corpses of the spruce. But they were near the top, near the ridge.

Even the horses made a rush for the last bit. They had worked round to a scrap of spruce forest near the very top. They hurried in, out of the huge, monstrous, mechanical wind, that whistled inhumanly and was palely cold. So, stepping through the dark screen of trees, they emerged over the crest.

In front now was nothing but mountains, ponderous, massive, down-sitting mountains, in a huge and intricate knot, empty of life or soul. Under the bristling black feathers of spruce near-by lay patches of white snow. The lifeless valleys were concaves of rock and spruce, the rounded summits and the hog-backed summits of grey rock crowded one behind the other like some monstrous herd in arrest.

It frightened the Princess, it was *so* inhuman. She had not thought it could be so inhuman, so, as it were, anti-life. And yet now one of her desires was fulfilled. She had seen it, the massive, gruesome, repellent core of the Rockies. She saw it there beneath her eyes, in its gigantic, heavy gruesomeness.

And she wanted to go back. At this moment she wanted to turn back. She had looked down into the intestinal knot of these mountains. She was frightened. She wanted to go back.

But Romero was riding on, on the lee side of the spruce forest, above the concaves of the inner mountains. He turned round to her and pointed at the slope with a dark hand.

"Here a miner has been trying for gold," he said. It was a grey scratched-out heap near a hole – like a great badger hole. And it looked quite fresh.

"Quite lately?" said the Princess.

"No, long ago – twenty, thirty years." He had reined in his horse and was looking at the mountains. "Look!" he said. "There goes the Forest Service trail – along those ridges, on the top, way over there till it comes to Lucytown, where is the Goverment road. We go down there – no trail – see behind that mountain – you see the top, no trees, and some grass?"

His arm was lifted, his brown hand pointing, his dark eyes piercing into the distance, as he sat on his black horse twisting round to her. Strange and ominous, only the demon of himself, he seemed to her. She was dazed and a little sick, at that height, and she could not see any more. Only she saw an eagle turning in the air beyond, and the light from the west showed the pattern on him underneath.

"Shall I ever be able to go so far?" asked the Princess faintly, petulantly.

"Oh yes! All easy now. No more hard places."

They worked along the ridge, up and down, keeping on the lee side, the inner side, in the dark shadow. It was cold. Then the trail laddered up again, and they emerged on a narrow ridge-track, with the mountain slipping away enormously on either side. The Princess was afraid. For one moment she looked out, and saw the desert, the desert ridges, more desert, more blue ridges, shining pale and very vast, far below, vastly palely tilting to the western horizon. It was ethereal and terrifying in its gleaming, pale, half-burnished immensity, tilted at the west. She could not bear it. To the left was the ponderous, involved mass of mountains all kneeling heavily.

She closed her eyes and let her consciousness evaporate away. The mare followed the trail. So on and on, in the wind again.

They turned their backs to the wind, facing inwards to the mountains. She thought they had left the trail; it was quite invisible.

"No," he said, lifting his hand and pointing. "Don't you see the blazed trees?"

And making an effort of consciousness, she was able to perceive on a pale-grey dead spruce stem the old marks where an axe had chipped a piece away. But with the height, the cold, the wind, her brain was numb.

They turned again and began to descend; he told her they had left the trail. The horses slithered in the loose stones, picking their way downward. It was afternoon, the sun stood obtrusive and gleaming in the lower heavens – about four o'clock. The horses went steadily, slowly, but obstinately onwards. The air was getting colder. They were in among the lumpish peaks and steep concave valleys. She was barely conscious at all of Romero.

He dismounted and came to help her from her saddle. She tottered, but would not betray her feebleness.

"We must slide down here," he said. "I can lead the horses."

They were on a ridge, and facing a steep bare slope of pallid, tawny mountain grass on which the western sun shone full. It was steep and concave. The Princess felt she might start slipping, and go down like a toboggan into the great hollow.

But she pulled herself together. Her eye blazed up again with excitement and determination. A wind rushed past her; she could hear the shriek of spruce trees far below. Bright spots came on her cheeks as her hair blew across. She looked a wild, fairy-like little thing.

"No," she said. "I will take my horse."

"Then mind she doesn't slip down on top of you," said Romero. And away he went, nimbly dropping down the pale, steep incline, making from rock to rock, down the grass, and following any little slanting groove. His horse hopped and slithered after him, and sometimes stopped dead, with forefeet pressed back, refusing to go farther. He, below his horse, looked up and pulled the reins gently, and encouraged the creature. Then the horse once more dropped his forefeet with a jerk, and the descent continued.

The Princess set off in blind, reckless pursuit, tottering and yet nimble. And Romero, looking constantly back to see how she was faring, saw her fluttering down like some queer little bird, her orange breeches twinkling like the legs of some duck, and her head, tied in the blue and buff kerchief, bound round and round like the head of some blue-topped bird. The sorrel mare rocked and slipped behind her. But down came the Princess in a reckless intensity, a tiny, vivid spot on the great hollow flank of the tawny mountain. So tiny! Tiny as a frail bird's egg. It made Romero's mind go blank with wonder.

But they had to get down, out of that cold and dragging wind. The spruce trees stood below, where a tiny stream emerged in stones. Away plunged Romero, zigzagging down. And away behind, up the slope, fluttered the tiny, bright-coloured Princess, holding the end of the long reins, and leading the lumbering, four-footed, sliding mare.

At last they were down. Romero sat in the sun, below the wind, beside some squaw-berry bushes. The Princess came near, the colour flaming in her cheeks, her eyes dark blue, much darker than the kerchief on her head, and glowing unnaturally.

"We make it," said Romero.

"Yes," said the Princess, dropping the reins and subsiding on to the grass, unable to speak, unable to think.

But, thank heaven, they were out of the wind and in the sun.

In a few minutes her consciousness and her control began to come back. She drank a little water. Romero was attending to the saddles. Then they set off again, leading the horses still a little farther down the tiny stream-bed. Then they could mount.

They rode down a bank and into a valley grove dense with aspens. Winding through the thin, crowding, pale-smooth stems, the sun shone flickering beyond them, and the disc-like aspen leaves, waving queer mechanical signals, seemed to be splashing the gold light before her eyes. She rode on in a splashing dazzle of gold.

Then they entered shadow and the dark, resinous spruce trees. The fierce boughs always wanted to sweep her off her horse. She had to twist and squirm past.

But there was a semblance of an old trail. And all at once they emerged in the sun on the edge of the spruce grove, and there was a little cabin, and the bottom of a small, naked valley with grey rock and heaps of stones, and a round pool of intense green water, dark green. The sun was just about to leave it.

Indeed, as she stood, the shadow came over the cabin and over herself; they were in the lower gloom, a twilight. Above, the heights still blazed.

It was a little hole of a cabin, near the spruce trees, with an earthen floor and an unhinged door. There was a wooden bed-bunk, three old sawn-off log-lengths to sit on as stools, and a sort of fireplace; no room for anything else. The little hole would hardly contain two people. The roof had gone – but Romero had laid on thick spruce boughs.

The strange squalor of the primitive forest pervaded the place, the squalor of animals and their droppings, the squalor of the wild. The Princess knew the peculiar repulsiveness of it. She was tired and faint.

Romero hastily got a handful of twigs, set a little fire going in the stove grate, and went out to attend to the horses. The Princess vaguely, mechanically, put sticks on the fire, in a sort of stupor, watching the blaze, stupefied and fascinated. She could not make much fire – it would set the whole cabin alight. And smoke oozed out of the dilapidated mud-and-stone chimney.

When Romero came in with the saddle-pouches and saddles, hanging the saddles on the wall, there sat the little Princess on her stump of wood in front of the dilapidated fire-grate, warming her tiny hands at the blaze, while her oranges breeches glowed almost like another fire. She was in a sort of stupor.

"You have some whisky now, or some tea? Or wait for some soup?" he asked.

She rose and looked at him with bright, dazed eyes, half comprehending; the colour glowing hectic in her cheeks.

"Some tea," she said, "with a little whisky in it. Where's the kettle?"

"Wait," he said. "I'll bring the things."

She took her cloak from the back of her saddle, and followed him into the open. It was a deep cup of shadow. But above the sky was still shining, and the heights of the mountains were blazing with aspen like fire blazing.

Their horses were cropping the grass among the stones. Romero clambered up a heap of grey stones and began lifting away logs and rocks, till he had opened the mouth of one of the miner's little old workings. This was his cache. He brought out bundles of blankets, pans for cooking, a little petrol camp-stove, an axe, the regular camp outfit. He seemed so quick and energetic and full of force. This quick force dismayed the Princess a little.

She took a saucepan and went down the stones to the water. It was very still and mysterious, and of a deep green colour, yet pure, transparent as glass. How cold the place was! How mysterious and fearful.

She crouched in her dark cloak by the water, rinsing the saucepan, feeling the cold heavy above her, the shadow like a vast weight upon her, bowing her down. The sun was leaving the mountain-tops, departing, leaving her under profound shadow. Soon it would crush her down completely.

Sparks? Or eyes looking at her across the water? She gazed, hypnotised. And with her sharp eyes she made out in the dusk the pale form of a bob-cat crouching by the water's edge, pale as the stones among which it crouched, opposite. And it was watching her with cold, electric eyes of strange intentness, a sort of cold, icy wonder and fearlessness. She saw its *museau* pushed forward, its tufted ears pricking intensely up. It was watching her with cold, animal curiosity, something demonish and conscienceless.

She made a swift movement, spilling her water. And in a flash the creature was gone, leaping like a cat that is escaping; but strange and soft in its motion, with its little bob-tail. Rather fascinating. Yet that cold, intent, demonish watching! She shivered with cold and fear. She knew well enough the dread and repulsiveness of the wild.

Romero carried in the bundles of bedding and the camp outfit. The windowless cabin was already dark inside. He lit a lantern, and then went out again with the axe. She heard him chopping wood as she fed sticks to the fire under her water. When he came in with an armful of oak-scrub faggots, she had just thrown the tea into the water.

"Sit down," she said, "and drink tea."

He poured a little bootleg whisky into the enamel cups, and in the silence the two sat on the log-ends, sipping the hot liquid and coughing occasionally from the smoke.

"We burn these oak sticks," he said. "They don't make hardly any smoke."

Curious and remote he was, saying nothing except what had to be said. And she, for her part, was as remote from him. They seemed far, far apart, worlds apart, now they were so near.

He unwrapped one bundle of bedding, and spread the blankets and the sheepskin in the wooden bunk.

"You lie down and rest," he said, "and I make the supper."

She decided to do so. Wrapping her cloak round her, she lay down in the bunk, turning her face to the wall. She could hear him preparing supper over the little petrol stove. Soon she could smell the soup he was heating; and soon she heard the hissing of fried chicken in a pan.

"You eat your supper now?" he said.

With a jerky, despairing movement, she sat up in the bunk, tossing back her hair. She felt cornered.

"Give it me here," she said.

He handed her first the cupful of soup. She sat among the blankets, eating it slowly. She was hungry. Then he gave her an enamel plate with pieces of fried chicken and currant jelly, butter and bread. It was very good. As they ate the chicken he made the coffee. She said never a word. A certain resentment filled her. She was cornered.

When supper was over he washed the dishes, dried them, and put everything away carefully, else there would have been no room to move in the hole of a cabin. The oak-wood gave out a good bright heat.

He stood for a few moments at a loss. Then he asked her:

"You want to go to bed soon?"

"Soon," she said. "Where are you going to sleep?"

"I make my bed here—" he pointed to the floor along the wall. "Too cold out of doors."

"Yes," she said. "I suppose it is."

She sat immobile, her cheeks hot, full of conflicting thoughts. And she watched him while he folded the blankets on the floor, a sheepskin underneath. Then she went out into night.

The stars were big. Mars sat on the edge of a mountain, for all the world like the blazing eye of a crouching mountain lion. But she herself was deep, deep below in a pit of shadow. In the intense silence she seemed to hear the spruce forest crackling with electricity and cold. Strange, foreign stars floated on that unmoving water. The night was going to freeze. Over the hills came the far sobbing-singing howling of the coyotes. She wondered how the horses would be.

Shuddering a little, she turned to the cabin. Warm light showed through its chinks. She pushed at the rickety, half-opened door.

"What about the horses?" she said.

"My black, he won't go away. And your mare will stay with him. You want to go to bed now?"

"I think I do."

"All right. I feed the horses some oats."

And he went out into the night.

He did not come back for some time. She was lying wrapped up tight in the bunk.

He blew out the lantern, and sat down on his bedding to take off his clothes. She lay with her back turned. And soon, in the silence, she was asleep.

She dreamed it was snowing, and the snow was falling on her through the roof, softly, softly, helplessly, and she was going to be buried alive. She was growing colder and colder, the snow was weighing down on her. The snow was going to absorb her.

She awoke with a sudden convulsion, like pain. She was really very cold; perhaps the heavy blankets had numbed her. Her heart seemed unable to beat, she felt she could not move.

With another convulsion she sat up. It was intensely dark. There was not even a spark of fire, the light wood had burned right away. She sat in thick oblivious darkness. Only through a chink she could see a star.

What did she want? Oh, what did she want? She sat in bed and rocked herself woefully. She could hear the steady breathing of the sleeping man. She was shivering with cold; her heart seemed as if it could not beat. She wanted warmth, protection, she wanted to be taken away from herself. And at the same time, perhaps more deeply than anything, she wanted to keep herself intact, intact, untouched, that no one should have any power over her, or rights to her. It was a wild necessity in her that no one, particularly no man, should have any rights or power over her, that no one and nothing should possess her.

Yet that other thing! And she was so cold, so shivering, and her heart could not beat. Oh, would not someone help her heart to beat?

She tried to speak, and could not. Then she cleared her throat.

"Romero," she said strangely, "it is so cold."

Where did her voice come from, and whose voice was it, in the dark?

She heard him at once sit up, and his voice, startled, with a resonance that seemed to vibrate against her, saying:

"You want me to make you warm?"

"Yes."

As soon as he had lifted her in his arms, she wanted to scream to him not to touch her. She stiffened herself. Yet she was dumb.

And he was warm, but with a terrible animal warmth that seemed to annihilate her. He panted like an animal with desire. And she was given over to this thing.

She had never, never wanted to be given over to this. But she had *willed* that it should happen to her. And according to her will, she lay and let it happen. But she never wanted it. She never wanted to be thus assailed and handled, and mauled. She wanted to keep herself to herself.

However, she had willed it to happen, and it had happened. She panted with relief when it was over.

Yet even now she had to lie within the hard, powerful clasp of this other creature, this man. She dreaded to struggle to go away. She dreaded almost too much the icy cold of that other bunk.

"Do you want to go away from me?" asked his strange voice. Oh, if it could only have been a thousand miles away from her! Yet she had willed to have it thus close.

"No," she said.

And she could feel a curious joy and pride surging up again in him: at her expense. Because he had got her. She felt like a victim there. And he was exulting in his power over her, his possession, his pleasure.

When dawn came, he was fast asleep. She sat up suddenly.

"I want a fire," she said.

He opened his brown eyes wide, and smiled with a curious tender luxuriousness.

"I want you to make a fire," she said.

He glanced at the chinks of light. His brown face hardened to the day.

"All right," he said. "I'll make it."

She did her face while he dressed. She could not bear to look at him. He was so suffused with pride and luxury. She hid her face almost in despair. But feeling the cold blast of air as he opened the door, she wriggled down into the warm place where he had been. How soon the warmth ebbed, when he had gone!

He made a fire and went out, returning after a while with water.

"You stay in bed till the sun comes," he said. "It very cold."

"Hand me my cloak."

She wrapped the cloak fast round her, and sat up among the blankets. The warmth was already spreading from the fire.

"I suppose we will start back as soon as we've had breakfast?"

He was crouching at his camp-stove making scrambled eggs. He looked up suddenly, transfixed, and his brown eyes, so soft and luxuriously widened, looked straight at her.

"You want to?" he said.

"We'd better get back as soon as possible," she said, turning aside from his eyes.

"You want to get away from me?" he asked, repeating the question of the night in a sort of dread.

"I want to get away from here," she said decisively. And it was true. She wanted supremely to get away, back to the world of people.

He rose slowly to his feet, holding the aluminium frying-pan.

"Don't you like last night?" he asked.

"Not really," she said. "Why? Do you?"

He put down the frying-pan and stood staring at the wall. She could see she had given him a cruel blow. But she did not relent. She was getting her own back. She wanted to regain possession of all herself, and in some mysterious way she felt that he possessed some part of her still.

He looked round at her slowly, his face greyish and heavy.

"You Americans," he said, "you always want to do a man down."

"I am not American," she said. "I am British. And I don't want to do any man down. I only want to go back now."

"And what will you say about me, down there?"

"That you were very kind to me, and very good."

He crouched down again, and went on turning the eggs. He gave her her plate, and her coffee, and sat down to his own food.

But again he seemed not to be able to swallow. He looked up at her.

"You don't like last night?" he asked.

"Not really," she said, though with some difficulty. "I don't care for that kind of thing."

A blank sort of wonder spread over his face at these words, followed immediately by a black look of anger, and then a stony, sinister despair.

"You don't?" he said, looking her in the eyes.

"Not really," she replied, looking back with steady hostility into his eyes.

Then a dark flame seemed to come from his face.

"I make you," he said, as if to himself.

He rose and reached her clothes, that hung on a peg: the fine linen underwear, the orange breeches, the fleecy jumper, the blue-and-bluff kerchief; then he took up her riding-boots and her bead moccasins. Crushing everything in his arms, he opened the door. Sitting up, she saw him stride down to the dark-green pool in the frozen shadow of that deep cup of a valley. He tossed the clothing and the boots out on the pool. Ice had formed. And on the pure, dark green mirror, in the slaty shadow, the Princess saw her things lying, the white linen, the orange breeches, the black boots, the blue moccasins, a tangled heap of colour. Romero picked up rocks and heaved them out at the ice, till the surface broke and the fluttering clothing disappeared in the rattling water, while the valley echoed and shouted again with the sound.

She sat in despair among the blankets, hugging tight her pale-blue cloak. Romero strode straight back to the cabin.

"Now you stay here with me," he said.

She was furious. Her blue eyes met his. They were like two demons watching one another. In his face, beyond a sort of unrelieved gloom, was a demonish desire for death.

He saw her looking round the cabin, scheming. He saw her eyes on his rifle. He took the gun and went out with it. Returning, he pulled out her saddle, carried it to the tarn, and threw it in. Then he fetched his own saddle, and did the same.

"Now will you go away?" he said, looking at her with a smile.

She debated within herself whether to coax him and wheedle him. But she knew he was already beyond it. She sat among her blankets in a frozen sort of despair, hard as hard ice with anger.

He did the chores, and disappeared with the gun. She got up in her blue pyjamas, huddled in her cloak, and stood in the doorway. The dark-green pool was motionless again, the stony slopes were pallid and frozen. Shadow still lay, like an after-death, deep in this valley. Always in the distance she saw the horses feeding.

If she could catch one! The brilliant yellow sun was half-way down the mountain. It was nine o'clock.

All day she was alone, and she was frightened. What she was frightened of she didn't know. Perhaps the crackling in the dark spruce wood. Perhaps just the savage, heartless wildness of the mountains. But all day she sat in the sun in the doorway of the cabin, watching, watching for hope. And all the time her bowels were cramped with fear.

She saw a dark spot that probably was a bear, roving across the pale grassy slope in the far distance, in the sun.

When, in the afternoon, she saw Romero approaching, with silent suddenness, carrying his gun and a dead deer, the cramp in her bowels relaxed, then became colder. She dreaded him with a cold dread.

"There is deer-meat," he said, throwing the dead doe at her feet.

"You don't want to go away from here," he said. "This is a nice place."

She shrank into the cabin.

"Come into the sun," he said, following her. She looked up at him with hostile, frightened eyes.

"Come into the sun," he repeated, taking her gently by the arm, in a powerful grasp.

She knew it was useless to rebel. Quietly he led her out, and seated himself in the doorway, holding her still by the arm.

"In the sun it is warm," he said. "Look, this is a nice place. You are such a pretty white woman, why do you want to act mean to me? Isn't this a nice place? Come! Come here! It is sure warm here."

He drew her to him, and in spite of her stony resistance, he took her cloak from her, holding her in her thin blue pyjamas.

"You sure are a pretty little white woman, small and pretty," he said. "You sure won't act mean to me – you don't want to, I know you don't."

She, stony and powerless, had to submit to him. The sun shone on her white, delicate skin.

"I sure don't mind hell fire," he said. "After this."

A queer, luxurious good humour seemed to possess him again. But though outwardly she was powerless, inwardly she resisted him, absolutely and stonily.

When later he was leaving her again, she said to him suddenly:

"You think you can conquer me this way. But you can't. You can never conquer me."

He stood arrested, looking back at her, with many emotions conflicting in his face – wonder, surprise, a touch of horror, and an unconscious pain that crumpled his face till it was like a mask. Then he went out without saying a word, hung the dead deer on a bough, and started to flay it. While he was at this butcher's work, the sun sank and cold night came on again.

"You see," he said to her as he crouched, cooking the supper, "I ain't going to let you go. I reckon you called to me in the night, and I've some right. If you want to fix it up right now with me, and say you want to be with me, we'll fix it up now and go down to the ranch to-morrow and get married or whatever you want. But you've got to say you want to be with me. Else I shall stay right here, till something happens."

She waited a while before she answered:

"I don't want to be with anybody against my will. I don't dislike you; at least, I didn't, till you tried to put your will over mine. I won't have anybody's will put over me. You can't succeed. Nobody could. You can never get me under your will. And you won't have long to try, because soon they will send someone to look for me."

He pondered this last, and she regretted having said it. Then, sombre, he bent to the cooking again.

He could not conquer her, however much he violated her. Because her spirit was hard and flawless as a diamond. But he could shatter her. This she knew. Much more, and she would be shattered.

In a sombre, violent excess he tried to expend his desire for her. And she was racked with an agony, and felt each time she would die. Because, in some peculiar way, he had got hold of her, some unrealised part of her which she never wished to realise. Racked with a burning, tearing anguish, she felt that the thread of her being would break, and she would die. The burning heat that racked her inwardly.

If only, only she could be alone again, cool and intact! If only she could recover herself again, cool and intact! Would she ever, ever, ever be able to bear herself again?

Even now she did not hate him. It was beyond that. Like some racking, hot doom. Personally he hardly existed.

The next day he would not let her have any fire, because of attracting attention with the smoke. It was a grey day, and she was cold. He stayed round, and heated soup on the petrol stove. She lay motionless in the blankets.

And in the afternoon she pulled the clothes over her head and broke into tears. She had never really cried in her life. He dragged the blankets away and looked to see what was shaking her. She sobbed in helpless hysterics. He covered her over again and went outside, looking at the mountains, where clouds were dragging and leaving a little snow. It was a violent, windy, horrible day, the evil of winter rushing down.

She cried for hours. And after this a great silence came between them. They were two people who had died. He did not touch her any more. In the night she lay and shivered like a dying dog. She felt that her very shivering would rupture something in her body, and she would die.

At last she had to speak.

"Could you make a fire? I am so cold," she said, with chattering teeth.

"Want to come over here?" came his voice.

"I would rather you made me a fire," she said, her teeth knocking together and chopping the words in two.

He got up and kindled a fire. At last the warmth spread, and she could sleep.

The next day was still chilly, with some wind. But the sun shone. He went about in silence, with a dead-looking face. It was now so dreary and so like death she wished he would do anything rather than continue in this negation. If now he asked her to go down with him to the world and marry him, she would do it. What did it matter? Nothing mattered any more.

But he would not ask her. His desire was dead and heavy like ice within him. He kept watch around the house.

On the fourth day as she sat huddled in the doorway in the sun, hugged in a blanket, she saw two horsemen come over the crest of the grassy slope – small figures. She gave a cry. He looked up quickly and saw the figures. The men had dismounted. They were looking for the trail.

"They are looking for me," she said.

"*Muy bien*," he answered in Spanish.

He went and fetched his gun, and sat with it across his knees.

"Oh!" she said. "Don't shoot!"

He looked across at her.

"Why?" he said. "You like staying with me?"

"No," she said. "But don't shoot."

"I ain't going to Pen," he said.

"You won't have to go to Pen," she said. "Don't shoot!"

"I'm going to shoot," he muttered.

And straightaway he kneeled and took very careful aim. The Princess sat on in an agony of helplessness and hopelessness.

The shot rang out. In an instant she saw one of the horses on the pale grassy slope rear and go rolling down. The man had dropped in the grass, and was invisible. The second man clambered on his horse, and on that precipitous place went at a gallop in a long swerve towards the nearest spruce tree cover. Bang! Bang! Went Romero's shots. But each time he missed, and the running horse leaped like a kangaroo towards cover.

It was hidden. Romero now got behind a rock; tense silence, in the brilliant sunshine. The Princess sat on the bunk inside the cabin, crouching, paralysed. For hours, it seemed, Romero knelt behind this rock, in his black shirt, bare-headed, watching. He had a beautiful, alert figure. The Princess wondered why she did not feel sorry for him. But her spirit was hard and cold, her heart could not melt. Though now she would have called him to her, with love.

But no, she did not love him. She would never love any man. Never! It was fixed and sealed in her, almost vindictively.

Suddenly she was so startled she almost fell from the bunk. A shot rang out quite close from behind the cabin. Romero leaped straight into the air, his arms fell outstretched, turning as he leaped. And even while he was in the air, a second shot rang out, and he fell with a crash, squirming, his hands clutching the earth towards the cabin door.

The Princess sat absolutely motionless, transfixed, staring at the prostrate figure. In a few moments the figure of a man in the Forest Service appeared close to the house; a young man in a broad-brimmed Stetson hat, dark flannel shirt, and riding-boots, carrying a gun. He strode over to the prostrate figure.

"Got you, Romero!" he said aloud. And he turned the dead man over. There was already a little pool of blood where Romero's breast had been.

"H'm!" said the Forest Service man. "Guess I got you nearer than I thought."

And he squatted there, staring at the dead man.

The distant calling of his comrade aroused him. He stood up.

"Hullo, Bill!" he shouted. "Yep! Got him! Yep! Done him in, apparently."

The second man rode out of the forest on a grey horse. He had a ruddy, kind face, and round brown eyes, dilated with dismay.

"He's not passed out?" he asked anxiously.

"Looks like it," said the first young man coolly.

The second dismounted and bent over the body. Then he stood up again, and nodded.

"Yea-a!" he said. "He's done in all right. It's him all right, boy! It's Domingo Romero."

"Yep! I know it!" replied the other.

Then in perplexity he turned and looked into the cabin, where the Princess squatted, staring with big owl eyes from her red blanket.

"Hello!" he said, coming towards the hut. And he took his hat off. Oh, the sense of ridicule she felt! Though he did not mean any.

But she could not speak, no matter what she felt.

"What'd this man start firing for?" he asked.

She fumbled for words, with numb lips.

"He had gone out of his mind!" she said, with solemn, stammering conviction.

"Good Lord! You mean to say he'd gone out of his mind? Whew! That's pretty awful! That explains it then. H'm!"

He accepted the explanation without more ado.

With some difficulty they succeeded in getting the Princess down to the ranch. But she, too, was not a little mad.

"I'm not quite sure where I am," she said to Mrs. Wilkieson, as she lay in bed. "Do you mind explaining?"

Mrs. Wilkieson explained tactfully.

"Oh yes!" said the Princess. "I remember. And I had an accident in the mountains, didn't I? Didn't we meet a man who'd gone mad, and who shot my horse from under me?"

"Yes, you met a man who had gone out of his mind."

The real affair was hushed up. The Princess departed east in a fortnight's time, in Miss Cummins's care. Apparently she had recovered herself entirely. She was the Princess, and a virgin intact.

But her bobbed hair was grey at the temples, and her eyes were a little mad. She was slightly crazy.

"Since my accident in the mountains, when a man went mad and shot my horse from under me, and my guide had to shoot him dead, I have never felt quite myself."

So she put it.

Later, she married an elderly man, and seemed pleased.

STORY 2
THE BLACK CAT

Edgar Allan Poe

For the most wild, yet most homely narrative which I am about to pen, I neither expect nor solicit belief. Mad indeed would I be to expect it, in a case where my very senses reject their own evidence. Yet, mad am I not – and very surely do I not dream. But to-morrow I die, and to-day I would unburthen my soul. My immediate purpose is to place before the world, plainly, succinctly, and without comment, a series of mere household events. In their consequences, these events have terrified – have tortured – have destroyed me. Yet I will not attempt to expound them. To me, they have presented little but Horror – to many they will seem less terrible than *barroques*. Hereafter, perhaps, some intellect may be found which will reduce my phantasm to the common-place – some intellect more calm, more logical, and far less excitable than my own, which will perceive, in the circumstances I detail with awe, nothing more than an ordinary succession of very natural causes and effects.

From my infancy I was noted for the docility and humanity of my disposition. My tenderness of heart was even so conspicuous as to make me the jest of my companions. I was especially fond of animals, and was indulged by my parents with a great variety of pets. With these I spent most of my time, and never was so happy as when feeding and caressing them. This peculiarity of character grew with my growth, and in my manhood, I derived from it one of my principal sources of pleasure. To those who have cherished an affection for a faithful and sagacious dog, I need hardly be at the trouble of explaining the nature or the intensity of the gratification thus derivable. There is something in the unselfish and self-sacrificing love of a brute, which goes directly to the heart of him who has had frequent occasion to test the paltry friendship and gossamer fidelity of mere *Man*.

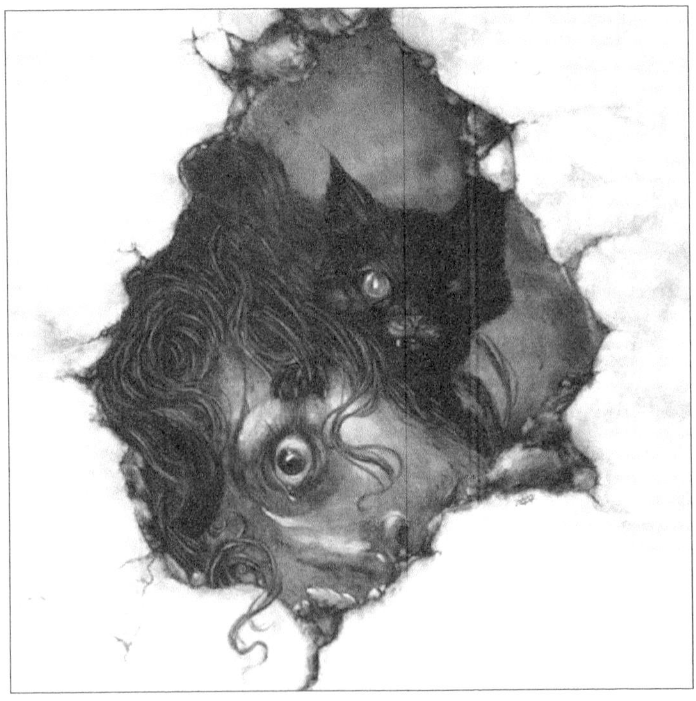

I married early, and was happy to find in my wife a disposition not uncongenial with my own. Observing my partiality for domestic pets, she lost no opportunity of procuring those of the most agreeable kind. We had birds, gold-fish, a fine dog, rabbits, a small monkey, and *a cat*.

This latter was a remarkably large and beautiful animal, entirely black, and sagacious to an astonishing degree. In speaking of his intelligence, my wife, who at heart was not a little tinctured with superstition, made frequent allusion to the ancient popular notion, which regarded all black cats as witches in disguise. Not that she was ever *serious* upon this point – and I mention the matter at all for no better reason than that it happens, just now, to be remembered.

Pluto – this was the cat's name – was my favorite pet and playmate. I alone fed him, and he attended me wherever I went about the house. It was even with difficulty that I could prevent him from following me through the streets.

Our friendship lasted, in this manner, for several years, during which my general temperament and character – through the instrumentality of the Fiend Intemperance – had (I blush to confess it) experienced a radical alteration for the worse. I grew, day by day, more moody, more irritable, more regardless of the feelings of others. I suffered myself to use intemperate language to my wife. At length, I even offered her personal violence. My pets, of course, were made to feel the change in my disposition. I not only neglected, but ill-used them. For Pluto, however, I still retained sufficient regard to restrain me from maltreating him, as I made no scruple of maltreating the rabbits, the monkey, or even the dog, when by accident, or through affection, they came in my way. But my disease grew upon me – for what disease is like Alcohol! – and at length even Pluto, who was now becoming old, and consequently somewhat peevish – even Pluto began to experience the effects of my ill temper.

One night, returning home, much intoxicated, from one of my haunts about town, I fancied that the cat avoided my presence. I seized him; when, in his fright at my violence, he inflicted a slight wound upon my hand with his teeth. The fury of a demon instantly possessed me. I knew myself no longer. My original soul seemed, at once, to take its flight from my body and a more than fiendish malevolence, gin-nurtured, thrilled every fibre of my frame. I took from my waistcoat-pocket a pen-knife, opened it, grasped the poor beast by the throat, and deliberately cut one of its eyes from the socket! I blush, I burn, I shudder, while I pen the damnable atrocity.

When reason returned with the morning – when I had slept off the fumes of the night's debauch – I experienced a sentiment half of horror, half of remorse, for the crime of which I had been guilty; but it was, at best, a feeble and equivocal feeling, and the soul remained untouched. I again plunged into excess, and soon drowned in wine all memory of the deed.

In the meantime the cat slowly recovered. The socket of the lost eye presented, it is true, a frightful appearance, but he no longer appeared to suffer any pain. He went about the house as usual, but, as might be expected, fled in extreme terror at my approach. I had so much of my old heart left, as to be at first grieved by this evident dislike on the part of a creature which had once so loved me. But this feeling soon gave place to irritation. And then came, as if to my final and irrevocable overthrow, the spirit of PERVERSENESS. Of this spirit philosophy takes no account. Yet I am not more sure that my soul lives, than I am that perverseness is one of the primitive impulses of the human heart – one of the indivisible primary faculties, or sentiments, which give direction to the character of Man. Who has not, a hundred times, found himself committing a vile or a silly action, for no other reason than because he knows he should not? Have we not a perpetual inclination, in the teeth of our best judgment, to violate that which is *Law*, merely because we understand it to be such? This spirit of perverseness, I say, came to my final overthrow. It was this unfathomable longing of the soul *to vex itself* – to offer violence to its own nature – to do wrong for the wrong's sake only – that urged me to continue and finally to consummate the injury I had inflicted upon the unoffending brute. One morning, in cool blood, I slipped a noose about its neck and hung it to the limb of a tree; – hung it with the tears streaming from my eyes, and with the bitterest remorse at my heart; – hung it *because* I knew that it had loved me, and *because* I felt it had given me no reason of offence; – hung it *because* I knew that in so doing I was committing a sin – a deadly sin that would so jeopardize my immortal soul as to place it – if such a thing wore possible – even beyond the reach of the infinite mercy of the Most Merciful and Most Terrible God.

On the night of the day on which this cruel deed was done, I was aroused from sleep by the cry of fire. The curtains of my bed were in flames. The whole house was blazing. It was with great difficulty that my wife, a servant, and myself, made our escape from the conflagration. The destruction was complete. My entire worldly wealth was swallowed up, and I resigned myself thenceforward to despair.

I am above the weakness of seeking to establish a sequence of cause and effect, between the disaster and the atrocity. But I am detailing a chain of facts – and wish not to leave even a possible link imperfect. On the day succeeding the fire, I visited the ruins. The walls, with one exception, had fallen in. This exception was found in a compartment wall, not very thick, which stood about the middle of the house, and against which had rested the head of my bed. The plastering had here, in great measure, resisted the action of the fire – a fact which I attributed to its having been recently spread. About this wall a dense crowd were collected, and many persons seemed to be examining a particular portion of it with very minute and eager attention. The words "strange!" "singular!" and other similar expressions, excited my curiosity. I approached and saw, as if graven in *bas relief* upon the white surface, the figure of a gigantic *cat*. The impression was given with an accuracy truly marvellous. There was a rope about the animal's neck.

When I first beheld this apparition – for I could scarcely regard it as less – my wonder and my terror were extreme. But at length reflection came to my aid. The cat, I remembered, had been hung in a garden adjacent to the house. Upon the alarm of fire, this garden had been immediately filled by the crowd – by some one of whom the animal must have been cut from the tree and thrown, through an open window, into my chamber. This had probably been done with the view of arousing me from sleep. The falling of other walls had compressed the victim of my cruelty into the substance of the freshly-spread plaster; the lime of which, with the flames, and the *ammonia* from the carcass, had then accomplished the portraiture as I saw it.

Although I thus readily accounted to my reason, if not altogether to my conscience, for the startling fact just detailed, it did not the less fail to make a deep impression upon my fancy. For months I could not rid myself of the phantasm of the cat; and, during this period, there came back into my spirit a half-sentiment that seemed, but was not, remorse. I went so far as to regret the loss of the animal, and to look about me, among the vile haunts which I now habitually frequented, for another pet of the same species, and of somewhat similar appearance, with which to supply its place.

One night as I sat, half stupified, in a den of more than infamy, my attention was suddenly drawn to some black object, reposing upon the head of one of the immense hogsheads of Gin, or of Rum, which constituted the chief furniture of the apartment. I had been looking steadily at the top of this hogshead for some minutes, and what now caused me surprise was the fact that I had not sooner perceived the object thereupon. I approached it, and touched it with my hand. It was a black cat – a very large one – fully as large as Pluto, and closely resembling him in every respect but one. Pluto had not a white hair upon any portion of his body; but this cat had a large, although indefinite splotch of white, covering nearly the whole region of the breast. Upon my touching him, he immediately arose, purred loudly, rubbed against my hand, and appeared delighted with my notice. This, then, was the very creature of which I was in search. I at once offered to purchase it of the landlord; but this person made no claim to it – knew nothing of it – had never seen it before.

I continued my caresses, and, when I prepared to go home, the animal evinced a disposition to accompany me. I permitted it to do so; occasionally stooping and patting it as I proceeded. When it reached the house it domesticated itself at once, and became immediately a great favorite with my wife.

For my own part, I soon found a dislike to it arising within me. This was just the reverse of what I had anticipated; but – I know not how or why it was – its evident fondness for myself rather disgusted and annoyed. By slow degrees, these feelings of disgust and annoyance rose into the bitterness of hatred. I avoided the creature; a certain sense of shame, and the remembrance of my former deed of cruelty, preventing me from physically abusing it. I did not, for some weeks, strike, or otherwise violently ill use it; but gradually – very gradually – I came to look upon it with unutterable loathing, and to flee silently from its odious presence, as from the breath of a pestilence.

What added, no doubt, to my hatred of the beast, was the discovery, on the morning after I brought it home, that, like Pluto, it also had been deprived of one of its eyes. This circumstance, however, only endeared it to my wife, who, as I have already said, possessed, in a high degree, that humanity of feeling which had once been my distinguishing trait, and the source of many of my simplest and purest pleasures.

With my aversion to this cat, however, its partiality for myself seemed to increase. It followed my footsteps with a pertinacity which it would be difficult to make the reader comprehend. Whenever I sat, it would crouch beneath my chair, or spring upon my knees, covering me with its loathsome caresses. If I arose to walk it would get between my feet and thus nearly throw me down, or, fastening its long and sharp claws in my dress, clamber, in this manner, to my breast. At such times, although I longed to destroy it with a blow, I was yet withheld from so doing, partly by a memory of my former crime, but chiefly – let me confess it at once – by absolute dread of the beast.

This dread was not exactly a dread of physical evil – and yet I should be at a loss how otherwise to define it. I am almost ashamed to own – yes, even in this felon's cell, I am almost ashamed to own – that the terror and horror with which the animal inspired me, had been heightened by one of the merest chimaeras it would be possible to conceive. My wife had called my attention, more than once, to the character of the mark of white hair, of which I have spoken, and which constituted the sole visible difference between the strange beast and the one I had destroyed. The reader will remember that this mark, although large, had been originally very indefinite; but, by slow degrees – degrees nearly imperceptible, and which for a long time my Reason struggled to reject as fanciful – it had, at length, assumed a rigorous distinctness of outline. It was now the representation of an object that I shudder to name – and for this, above all, I loathed, and dreaded, and would have rid myself of the monster *had I dared* – it was now, I say, the image of a hideous – of a ghastly thing – of the GALLOWS! – oh, mournful and terrible engine of Horror and of Crime – of Agony and of Death!

And now was I indeed wretched beyond the wretchedness of mere Humanity. And *a brute beast* – whose fellow I had contemptuously destroyed – *a brute beast* to work out for *me* – for me a man, fashioned in the image of the High God – so much of insufferable wo! Alas! Neither by day nor by night knew I the blessing of Rest any more! During the former the creature left me no moment alone; and, in the latter, I started, hourly, from dreams of unutterable fear, to find the hot breath of *the thing* upon my face, and its vast weight – an incarnate Night-Mare that I had no power to shake off – incumbent eternally upon my *heart!*

Beneath the pressure of torments such as these, the feeble remnant of the good within me succumbed. Evil thoughts became my sole intimates – the darkest and most evil of thoughts. The moodiness of my usual temper increased to hatred of all things and of all mankind; while, from the sudden, frequent, and ungovernable outbursts of a fury to which I now blindly abandoned myself, my uncomplaining wife, alas! was the most usual and the most patient of sufferers.

One day she accompanied me, upon some household errand, into the cellar of the old building which our poverty compelled us to inhabit. The cat followed me down the steep stairs, and, nearly throwing me headlong, exasperated me to madness. Uplifting an axe, and forgetting, in my wrath, the childish dread which had hitherto stayed my hand, I aimed a blow at the animal which, of course, would have proved instantly fatal had it descended as I wished. But this blow was arrested by the hand of my wife. Goaded, by the interference, into a rage more than demoniacal, I withdrew my arm from her grasp and buried the axe in her brain. She fell dead upon the spot, without a groan.

This hideous murder accomplished, I set myself forthwith, and with entire deliberation, to the task of concealing the body. I knew that I could not remove it from the house, either by day or by night, without the risk of being observed by the neighbors. Many projects entered my mind. At one period I thought of cutting the corpse into minute fragments, and destroying them by fire. At another, I resolved to dig a grave for it in the floor of the cellar. Again, I deliberated about casting it in the well in the yard – about packing it in a box, as if merchandize, with the usual arrangements, and so getting a porter to take it from the house. Finally I hit upon what I considered a far better expedient than either of these. I determined to wall it up in the cellar – as the monks of the middle ages are recorded to have walled up their victims.

For a purpose such as this the cellar was well adapted. Its walls were loosely constructed, and had lately been plastered through-out with a rough plaster, which the dampness of the atmosphere had prevented from hardening. Moreover, in one of the walls was a projection, caused by a false chimney, or fireplace, that had been filled up, and made to resemble the red of the cellar.

I made no doubt that I could readily displace the bricks at this point, insert the corpse, and wall the whole up as before, so that no eye could detect anything suspicious. And in this calculation I was not deceived. By means of a crow-bar I easily dislodged the bricks, and, having carefully deposited the body against the inner wall, I propped it in that position, while, with little trouble, I re-laid the whole structure as it originally stood. Having procured mortar, sand, and hair, with every possible precaution, I prepared a plaster which could not be distinguished from the old, and with this I very carefully went over the new brickwork. When I had finished, I felt satisfied that all was right. The wall did not present the slightest appearance of having been disturbed. The rubbish on the floor was picked up with the minutest care. I looked around triumphantly, and said to myself – "Here at least, then, my labor has not been in vain."

My next step was to look for the beast which had been the cause of so much wretchedness; for I had, at length, firmly resolved to put it to death. Had I been able to meet with it, at the moment, there could have been no doubt of its fate; but it appeared that the crafty animal had been alarmed at the violence of my previous anger, and forebore to present itself in my present mood. It is impossible to describe, or to imagine, the deep, the blissful sense of relief which the absence of the detested creature occasioned in my bosom. It did not make its appearance during the night – and thus for one night at least, since its introduction into the house, I soundly and tranquilly slept; aye, slept even with the burden of murder upon my soul!

The second and the third day passed, and still my tormentor came not. Once again I breathed as a freeman. The monster, in terror, had fled the premises forever! I should behold it no more! My happiness was supreme! The guilt of my dark deed disturbed me but little. Some few inquiries had been made, but these had been readily answered. Even a search had been instituted – but of course nothing was to be discovered. I looked upon my future felicity as secured.

Upon the fourth day of the assassination, a party of the police came, very unexpectedly, into the house, and proceeded again to make rigorous investigation of the premises. Secure, however, in the inscrutability of my place of concealment, I felt no embarrassment whatever. The officers bade me accompany them in their search. They left no nook or corner unexplored. At length, for the third or fourth time, they descended into the cellar. I quivered not in a muscle. My heart beat calmly as that of one who slumbers in innocence. I walked the cellar from end to end. I folded my arms upon my bosom, and roamed easily to and fro. The police were thoroughly satisfied and prepared to depart. The glee at my heart was too strong to be restrained. I burned to say if but one word, by way of triumph, and to render doubly sure their assurance of my guiltlessness.

"Gentlemen," I said at last, as the party ascended the steps, "I delight to have allayed your suspicions. I wish you all health, and a little more courtesy. By the bye, gentlemen, this – this is a very well constructed house." [In the rabid desire to say something easily, I scarcely knew what I uttered at all.] – "I may say an *excellently* well constructed house. These walls – are you going, gentlemen? – these walls are solidly put together;" and here, through the mere phrenzy of bravado, I rapped heavily, with a cane which I held in my hand, upon that very portion of the brick-work behind which stood the corpse of the wife of my bosom.

But may God shield and deliver me from the fangs of the Arch-Fiend! No sooner had the reverberation of my blows sunk into silence, than I was answered by a voice from within the tomb! –

by a cry, at first muffled and broken, like the sobbing of a child, and then quickly swelling into one long, loud, and continuous scream, utterly anomalous and inhuman – a howl – a wailing shriek, half of horror and half of triumph, such as might have arisen only out of hell, conjointly from the throats of the dammed in their agony and of the demons that exult in the damnation.

Of my own thoughts it is folly to speak. Swooning, I staggered to the opposite wall. For one instant the party upon the stairs remained motionless, through extremity of terror and of awe. In the next, a dozen stout arms were toiling at the wall. It fell bodily. The corpse, already greatly decayed and clotted with gore, stood erect before the eyes of the spectators. Upon its head, with red extended mouth and solitary eye of fire, sat the hideous beast whose craft had seduced me into murder, and whose informing voice had consigned me to the hangman. I had walled the monster up within the tomb!

STORY 3

THE OTHER SIDE OF THE HEDGE

EM Forster

My pedometer told me that I was twenty-five; and, though it is a shocking thing to stop walking, I was so tired that I sat down on a milestone to rest. People outstripped me, jeering as they did so, but I was too apathetic to feel resentful, and even when Miss Eliza Dimbleby, the great educationist, swept past, exhorting me to persevere, I only smiled and raised my hat.

At first I thought I was going to be like my brother, whom I had had to leave by the road-side a year or two round the corner. He had wasted his breath on singing, and his strength on helping others. But I had travelled more wisely, and now it was only the monotony of the highway that oppressed me – dust under foot and brown crackling hedges on either side, ever since I could remember.

And I had already dropped several things – indeed, the road behind was strewn with the things we all had dropped; and the white dust was settling down on them, so that already they looked no better than stones. My muscles were so weary that I could not even bear the weight of those things I still carried. I slid off the milestone into the road, and lay there prostrate, with my face to the great parched hedge, praying that I might give up.

A little puff of air revived me. It seemed to come from the hedge; and, when I opened my eyes, there was a glint of light through the tangle of boughs and dead leaves. The hedge could not be as thick as usual. In my weak, morbid state, I longed to force my way in, and see what was on the other side. No one was in sight, or I should not have dared to try. For we of the road do not admit in conversation that there is another side at all.

I yielded to the temptation, saying to myself that I would come back in a minute. The thorns scratched my face, and I had to use my arms as a shield, depending on my feet alone to push me forward. Halfway through I would have gone back, for in the passage all the things I was carrying were scraped off me, and my clothes were torn. But I was so wedged that return was impossible, and I had to wriggle blindly forward, expecting every moment that my strength would fail me, and that I should perish in the undergrowth.

Suddenly cold water closed round my head, and I seemed sinking down for ever. I had fallen out of the hedge into a deep pool. I rose to the surface at last, crying for help, and I heard someone on the opposite bank laugh and say: "Another!" And then I was twitched out and laid panting on the dry ground.

Even when the water was out of my eyes, I was still dazed, for I had never been in so large a space, nor seen such grass and sunshine. The blue sky was no longer a strip, and beneath it the earth had risen grandly into hills – clean, bare buttresses, with beech trees in their folds, and meadows and clear pools at their feet. But the hills were not high, and there was in the landscape a sense of human occupation – so that one might have called it a park, or garden, if the words did not imply a certain triviality and constraint.

As soon as I got my breath, I turned to my rescuer and said:

"Where does this place lead to?"

"Nowhere, thank the Lord!" said he, and laughed. He was a man of fifty or sixty – just the kind of age we mistrust on the road – but there was no anxiety in his manner, and his voice was that of a boy of eighteen.

"But it must lead somewhere!" I cried, too much surprised at his answer to thank him for saving my life.

"He wants to know where it leads!" he shouted to some men on the hill side, and they laughed back, and waved their caps.

I noticed then that the pool into which I had fallen was really a moat which bent round to the left and to the right, and that the hedge followed it continually. The hedge was green on this side – its roots showed through the clear water, and fish swam about in them – and it was wreathed over with dog-roses and Traveller's Joy. But it was a barrier, and in a moment I lost all pleasure in the grass, the sky, the trees, the happy men and women, and realized that the place was but a prison, for all its beauty and extent.

We moved away from the boundary, and then followed a path almost parallel to it, across the meadows. I found it difficult walking, for I was always trying to out-distance my companion, and there was no advantage in doing this if the place led nowhere. I had never kept step with anyone since I left my brother.

I amused him by stopping suddenly and saying disconsolately, "This is perfectly terrible. One cannot advance: one cannot progress. Now we of the road——"

"Yes. I know."

"I was going to say, we advance continually."

"I know."

"We are always learning, expanding, developing. Why, even in my short life I have seen a great deal of advance – the Transvaal War, the Fiscal Question, Christian Science, Radium. Here for example—"

I took out my pedometer, but it still marked twenty-five, not a degree more.

"Oh, it's stopped! I meant to show you. It should have registered all the time I was walking with you. But it makes me only twenty-five."

"Many things don't work in here," he said, "One day a man brought in a Lee-Metford, and that wouldn't work."

"The laws of science are universal in their application. It must be the water in the moat that has injured the machinery. In normal conditions everything works. Science and the spirit of emulation – those are the forces that have made us what we are."

I had to break off and acknowledge the pleasant greetings of people whom we passed. Some of them were singing, some talking, some engaged in gardening, hay-making, or other rudimentary industries. They all seemed happy; and I might have been happy too, if I could have forgotten that the place led nowhere.

I was startled by a young man who came sprinting across our path, took a little fence in fine style, and went tearing over a ploughed field till he plunged into a lake, across which he began to swim. Here was true energy, and I exclaimed: "A cross-country race! Where are the others?"

"There are no others," my companion replied; and, later on, when we passed some long grass from which came the voice of a girl singing exquisitely to herself, he said again: "There are no others." I was bewildered at the waste in production, and murmured to myself, "What does it all mean?"

He said: "It means nothing but itself" – and he repeated the words slowly, as if I were a child.

"I understand," I said quietly, "but I do not agree. Every achievement is worthless unless it is a link in the chain of development. And I must not trespass on your kindness any longer. I must get back somehow to the road, and have my pedometer mended."

"First, you must see the gates," he replied, "for we have gates, though we never use them."

I yielded politely, and before long we reached the moat again, at a point where it was spanned by a bridge. Over the bridge was a big gate, as white as ivory, which was fitted into a gap in the boundary hedge. The gate opened outwards, and I exclaimed in amazement, for from it ran a road – just such a road as I had left – dusty under foot, with brown crackling hedges on either side as far as the eye could reach.

"That's my road!" I cried.

He shut the gate and said: "But not your part of the road. It is through this gate that humanity went out countless ages ago, when it was first seized with the desire to walk."

I denied this, observing that the part of the road I myself had left was not more than two miles off. But with the obstinacy of his years he repeated: "It is the same road. This is the beginning, and though it seems to run straight away from us, it doubles so often, that it is never far from our boundary and sometimes touches it." He stooped down by the moat, and traced on its moist margin an absurd figure like a maze. As we walked back through the meadows, I tried to convince him of his mistake.

"The road sometimes doubles, to be sure, but that is part of our discipline. Who can doubt that its general tendency is onward? To what goal we know not – it may be to some mountain where we shall touch the sky, it may be over precipices into the sea. But that it goes forward – who can doubt that? It is the thought of that that makes us strive to excel, each in his own way, and gives us an impetus which is lacking with you. Now that man who passed us – it's true that he ran well, and jumped well, and swam well; but we have men who can run better, and men who can jump better, and who can swim better. Specialization has produced results which would surprise you. Similarly, that girl——"

Here I interrupted myself to exclaim: "Good gracious me! I could have sworn it was Miss Eliza Dimbleby over there, with her feet in the fountain!"

He believed that it was.

"Impossible! I left her on the road, and she is due to lecture this evening at Tunbridge Wells. Why, her train leaves Cannon Street in – of course my watch has stopped like everything else. She is the last person to be here."

"People always are astonished at meeting each other. All kinds come through the hedge, and come at all times – when they are drawing ahead in the race, when they are lagging behind, when they are left for dead. I often stand near the boundary listening to the sounds of the road – you know what they are – and wonder if anyone will turn aside. It is my great happiness to help someone out of the moat, as I helped you. For our country fills up slowly, though it was meant for all mankind."

"Mankind have other aims," I said gently, for I thought him well-meaning; "and I must join them." I bade him good evening, for the sun was declining, and I wished to be on the road by nightfall. To my alarm, he caught hold of me, crying: "You are not to go yet!" I tried to shake him off, for we had no interests in common, and his civility was becoming irksome to me. But for all my struggles the tiresome old man would not let go; and, as wrestling is not my speciality, I was obliged to follow him.

It was true that I could have never found alone the place where I came in, and I hoped that, when I had seen the other sights about which he was worrying, he would take me back to it. But I was determined not to sleep in the country, for I mistrusted it, and the people too, for all their friendliness. Hungry though I was, I would not join them in their evening meals of milk and fruit, and, when they gave me flowers, I flung them away as soon as I could do so unobserved. Already they were lying down for the night like cattle – some out on the bare hillside, others in groups under the beeches. In the light of an orange sunset I hurried on with my unwelcome guide, dead tired, faint for want of food, but murmuring indomitably: "Give me life, with its struggles and victories, with its failures and hatreds, with its deep moral meaning and its unknown goal!"

At last we came to a place where the encircling moat was spanned by another bridge, and where another gate interrupted the line of the boundary hedge. It was different from the first gate; for it was half transparent like horn, and opened inwards. But through it, in the waning light, I saw again just such a road as I had left – monotonous, dusty, with brown crackling hedges on either side, as far as the eye could reach.

I was strangely disquieted at the sight, which seemed to deprive me of all self-control. A man was passing us, returning for the night to the hills, with a scythe over his shoulder and a can of some liquid in his hand. I forgot the destiny of our race. I forgot the road that lay before my eyes, and I sprang at him, wrenched the can out of his hand, and began to drink.

It was nothing stronger than beer, but in my exhausted state it overcame me in a moment. As in a dream, I saw the old man shut the gate, and heard him say: "This is where your road ends, and through this gate humanity – all that is left of it – will come in to us."

Though my senses were sinking into oblivion, they seemed to expand ere they reached it. They perceived the magic song of nightingales, and the odour of invisible hay, and stars piercing the fading sky. The man whose beer I had stolen lowered me down gently to sleep off its effects, and, as he did so, I saw that he was my brother.

THE VILLAGE SCHOOLMASTER

Franz Kafka

Those, and I am one of them, who find even a small ordinary sized mole disgusting, would probably have died of disgust if they had seen the giant mole that a few years back was observed in the neighborhood of one of our villages, which achieved a certain transitory celebrity on account of the incident. Today it has long since sunk back into oblivion again, and in that only shares the obscurity of the whole incident, which has remained quite inexplicable, but which people, it must be confessed, have also taken no great pains to explain; and as a result of an incomprehensible apathy in those very circles that should have concerned themselves with it, and who in fact have shown enthusiastic interest in far more trifling matters, the affair has been forgotten without ever being adequately investigated. In any case, the fact that the village could not be reached by the railroad was no excuse. Many people came from great distances out of pure curiosity, there were even foreigners among them; it was only those who should have shown something more than curiosity that refrained from coming. In fact, if a few quite simple people, people whose daily work gave them hardly a moment of leisure if these people had not quite disinterestedly taken up the affair, the rumor of this natural phenomenon would probably have never spread beyond the locality. Indeed, rumor itself, which usually cannot be held within bounds, was actually sluggish in this case; if it had not literally been given a shove it would not have spread. But even that was no valid reason for re fusing to inquire into the affair; on the contrary this second phenomenon should have been investigated as well. Instead the old village schoolmaster was left to write the sole account in black and white of the incident, and though he was an excellent man in his own profession, neither his abilities nor his equipment made it possible for him to produce an exhaustive description that could be used as a foundation by others, far less, therefore, an actual explanation of the occurrence. His little pamphlet was printed, and a good many copies were sold to visitors to the village about that time; it also received some public recognition, but the teacher was wise enough to perceive that his fragmentary labors, in which no one supported him, were basically without value. If in spite of that he did not relax in them, and made the question his lifework, though it naturally became more hopeless from year to year, that only shows on the one hand how powerful an effect the appearance of the giant mole was capable of producing, and on the other how much laborious effort and fidelity to his convictions may be found in an old and obscure village schoolmaster. But that he suffered deeply from the cold attitude of the recognized authorities is proved by a brief brochure with which he followed up his pamphlet several years later, by which time hardly anyone could remember what it was all about. In this brochure he complained of the lack of understanding that he had encountered in people where it was least to be expected; complaints that carried conviction less by the skill with which they were expressed than by their honesty. Of such people he said very appositely: "It is not 1, but they, who talk like old village schoolmasters." And among other things he adduced the pronouncement of a scholar to whom he had gone expressly about his affair. The name of the scholar was not mentioned, but from various circumstances we could guess who it was. After the teacher had managed with great difficulty to secure admittance, he perceived at once from the very way in which he was greeted that the savant had already acquired a rooted prejudice against the matter. The absent-mindedness with which he listened to the long report which the teacher, pamphlet in hand, delivered to him, can be gauged from a remark that he let fall after a pause for ostensible reflection: "The soil in your neighborhood is particularly black and rich. Consequently it provides the moles with particularly rich nourishment, and so they grow to an unusual size."

"But not to such a size as that!" exclaimed the teacher, and he measured off two yards on the wall, somewhat exaggerating the length of the mole in exasperation. "Oh, and why not?" replied the scholar, who obviously looked upon the whole affair as a great joke. With this verdict the teacher had to return to his home. He tells how his wife and six children were waiting for him by the roadside in the snow, and how he had to admit to them the final collapse of his hopes.

When I read of the scholar's attitude toward the old man I was not yet acquainted with the teacher's pamphlet. But I at once resolved myself to collect and correlate all the information I could discover regarding the case. If I could not employ physical force against the scholar, I could at least write a defense of the teacher, or more exactly, of the good intentions of an honest but uninfluential man. I admit that I rued this decision later, for I soon saw that its execution was bound to involve me in a very strange predicament. On the one hand my own influence was far from sufficient to effect a change in learned or even public opinion in the teacher's favor, while on the other the teacher was bound to notice that I was less concerned with his main object, which was to prove that the giant mole had actually been seen, than to defend his honesty, which must naturally be self-evident to him and in need of no defense. Accordingly, what was bound to happen was this: I would be misunderstood by the teacher, though I wanted to collaborate with him, and instead of helping him I myself would probably require support, which was most unlikely to appear. Besides, my decision would impose a great burden of work upon me. If I wanted to convince people I could not invoke the teacher, since he himself had not been able to convince them. To read his pamphlet could only have led me astray, and so I refrained from reading it until I should have finished my own labors. More, I did not even get in touch with the teacher. True, he heard of my inquiries through intermediaries, but he did not know whether I was working for him or against him. In fact he probably assumed the latter, though he denied it later on; for I have proof of the fact that he put various obstacles in my way. It was quite easy for him to do that, for of course I was compelled to undertake anew all the inquiries he had already made, and so he could always steal a march on me

But that was the only objection that could be justly made to my method, an unavoidable reproach, but one that was palliated by the caution and self abnegation with which I drew my conclusions. But for the rest my pamphlet was quite uninfluenced by the teacher, perhaps on this point, indeed, I showed all too great a scrupulosity; from my words one might have thought nobody had ever inquired into the case before, and I was the first to interrogate those who had seen or heard of the mole, the first to correlate the evidence, the first to draw conclusions. When later I read the schoolmaster's pamphlet it had a very circumstantial title: "A mole, larger in size than ever seen before "I found that we actually did not agree on certain important points, though we both believed we had proved our main point, namely, the existence of the mole. These differences prevented the establishment of the friendly relations with the schoolmaster that I had been looking forward to in spite of everything. On his side there developed a feeling almost of hostility. True, he was always modest and humble in his bearing toward me, but that only made his real feelings the more obvious. In other words, he was of the opinion that I had merely damaged his credit, and that my belief that I had been or could be of assistance to him was simplicity at best, but more likely presumption or artifice. He was particularly fond of saying that all his previous enemies had shown their hostility either not at all, or in private, or at most by word of mouth, while I had considered it necessary to have my censures straightway published. Moreover, the few opponents of his who had really occupied themselves with the subject, if but superficially, had at least listened to his, the schoolmaster's, views before they had given expression to their own: while I, on the strength of unsystematically assembled and in part misunderstood evidence, had published conclusions which, even if they were correct as regarded the main point, must evoke incredulity, and among the public no less than the educated. But the faintest hint that the existence of the mole was unworthy of credence was the worst thing that could happen in this case.

To these reproaches, veiled as they were, I could easily have found an answer for instance, that his own pamphlet achieved the very summit of the incredible it was less easy, however, to make headway against his continual suspicion, and that was the reason why I was very reserved in my dealings with him. For in his heart he was convinced that I wanted to rob him of the fame of being the first man publicly to vindicate the mole. Now of course he really enjoyed no fame whatever, but only an absurd notoriety that was shrinking more and more, and for which I had certainly no desire to compete. Besides, in the foreword to my pamphlet I had expressly declared that the teacher must stand for all time as the discoverer of the mole and he was not even that and that only my sympathy with his unfortunate fate had spurred me on to write. "It is the aim of this pamphlet" so I ended up all too melodramatically, but it corresponded with my feelings at that time "to help in giving the schoolmaster's book the wide publicity it deserves. If I succeed in that, then may my name, which I regard as only transiently and indirectly associated with this question, be blotted from it at once." Thus I disclaimed expressly any major participation in the affair; it was almost as if I had foreseen in some manner the teacher's unbelievable reproaches. Nevertheless he found in that very passage a handle against me, and I do not deny that there was a faint show of justice in what he said or rather hinted; indeed I was often struck by the fact that he showed almost a keener penetration where I was concerned than he had done in his pamphlet. For he maintained that my foreword was double-faced. If I was really concerned solely to give publicity to his pamphlet, why had I not occupied myself exclusively with him and his pamphlet, why had I not pointed out its virtues, its irrefutability why had I not confined myself to insisting on the significance of the discovery and making that clear, why had I instead tackled the discovery itself, while completely ignoring the pamphlet? Had not the discovery been made already? Was there still anything left to be done in that direction? But if I really thought that it was necessary for me to make the discovery all over again, why had I disassociated myself from the discovery so solemnly in my foreword? One might put that down to false modesty, but it was something worse. I was trying to belittle the discovery, I was drawing attention to it merely for the purpose of depreciating it, while he on the other hand had inquired into and finally established it. Perhaps the affair had sunk somewhat into desuetude; now I had made a noise about it again, but at the same time I had made the schoolmaster's position more difficult than ever. What did he care whether his honesty was vindicated or not? All that he was concerned with was the thing itself, and with that alone. But I was only of disservice to it, for I did not understand it, I did not prize it at its true value, I had no real feeling for it. It was infinitely above my intellectual capacity. He sat before me and looked at me, his old wrinkled face quite composed, and yet this was what he was thinking. Yet it was not true that he was only concerned with the thing itself: actually he was very greedy for fame, and wanted to make money out of the business too, which, however, considering his large family, was very understandable. Nevertheless my interest in the affair seemed so trivial compared with his own, that he felt he could claim to be completely disinterested without deviating very seriously from the truth. And indeed my inner doubts refused to be quite calmed by my telling myself that the man's reproaches were really due to the fact that he clung to his mole, so to speak, with both hands, and was bound to look upon anyone who laid even a finger on it as a traitor. For that was not true; his attitude was not to be explained by greed, or at any rate by greed alone, but rather by the touchiness which his great labors and their complete unsuccess had bred in him.

Yet even his touchiness did not explain everything. Perhaps my interest in the affair was really too trivial. The schoolmaster was used to lack of interest in strangers. He regarded it as a universal evil, but no longer suffered from its individual manifestations. Now a man had appeared who, strangely enough, took up the affair; and even he did not understand it. Attacked from this side I can make no defense. I am no zoologist; yet perhaps I would have thrown myself into the case with my whole heart if I had discovered it; but I had not discovered it. Such a gigantic mole is certainly a prodigy, yet one cannot expect the continuous and undivided attention of the whole world to be accorded it, particularly if its existence is not completely and irrefutably established, and in any case it cannot be produced. And I admit too that even if I had been the discoverer I would probably never have come forward so gladly and voluntarily in defense of the mole as I had in that of the schoolmaster.

Now the misunderstanding between me and the schoolmaster would probably have quickly cleared up if my pamphlet had achieved success. But success was not forthcoming. Perhaps the book was not well enough written, not persuasive enough; I am a businessman, it may be that the composition of such a pamphlet was still further beyond my limited powers than those of the teacher, though in the kind of knowledge required I was greatly superior to him. Besides, my unsuccess may be explicable in other ways; the time at which the pamphlet appeared may have been inauspicious. The discovery of the mole, which had failed to penetrate to a wide public at the time it took place, was not so long past on the one hand as to be completely forgotten, and thus capable of being brought alive again by my pamphlet, while on the other hand enough time had elapsed quite to exhaust the trivial interest that had originally existed. Those who took my pamphlet at all seriously told themselves, in that bored tone which from the first had characterized the debate, that now the old useless labors on this wearisome question were to begin all over again; and some even confused my pamphlet with the schoolmasters In a leading agricultural journal appeared the following comment, fortunately at the very end, and in small _ print: "The pamphlet on the giant mole has once more been sent to us. Years ago we remember having had a hearty laugh over it. Since then it has not become more intelligible, nor we more hard of understanding. But we simply refuse to laugh at it a second time. Instead, we would ask our teaching associations whether more useful work cannot be found for our village schoolmasters than hunting out giant moles." An unpardonable confusion of identity. They had read neither the first nor the second pamphlet, and the two perfunctorily scanned expressions, "giant mole" and "village schoolmaster," were sufficient for these gentlemen, as representatives of publicly esteemed interest, to pronounce on the subject. Against this attack measures might have been attempted and with success, but the lack of understanding between the teacher and myself kept me from venturing upon them. I tried instead to keep the review from his knowledge as long as I could. But he very soon discovered it, as I recognized from a sentence in one of his letters, in which he announced his intention of visiting me for the Christmas holidays. He wrote: "The world is full of malice, and people smooth the path for it," by which he wished to convey that I was one of the malicious, but, not content with my own innate malice, wished also to make the world's path smooth for it: in other words, was acting in such a way as to arouse the general malice and help it to victory. Well, I summoned the resolution I required, and was able to await him calmly, and calmly greet him when he arrived, this time a shade less polite in his bearing than usual; he carefully drew out the journal from the breast pocket of his old-fashioned padded overcoat, and opening it handed it to me. "I've seen it," I replied, handing the journal back unread. "You've seen it," he said with a sigh; he had the old teacher's habit of repeating the other person's answers. "Of course I won't take this lying down!" he went on, tapping the journal excitedly with his finger and glancing up sharply at me, as if I were of a different mind; he certainly had some idea of what I was about to say, for I think I have noticed, not so much from his words as from other indications, that he often has a genuine intuition of my intentions, though he never yields to them but lets himself be diverted. What I said to him I can set down almost word for word, for I made a note of it shortly after our interview. "Do what you like," I said, "our ways part from this moment. I fancy that that is neither unexpected nor unwelcome news to you. The review in this journal is not the real reason for my decision; it has merely finally confirmed it. The real reason is this: originally I thought my intervention might be of some use to you, while now I cannot but recognize that I have damaged you in every direction. Why it has turned out so I cannot say; the causes of success and unsuccess are always ambiguous; but don't look for the sole explanation in my short-comings. Consider: you too had the best intentions, and yet, if one regards the matter objectively, you failed. I don't intend it as a joke, for it would be a joke against myself, when I say that your connection with me must unfortunately be counted among your failures. It is neither cowardice nor treachery, if I withdraw from the affair now. Actually it involves a certain degree of self renunciation; my pamphlet itself proves how much I respect you personally, in a certain sense you have become my teacher, and I have almost grown fond of the mole itself. Nevertheless I have decided to step aside; you are the discoverer, and all that I can do is to prevent you from gaining possible fame, while I attract failure and pass it on to you. At least that is your own opinion. Enough of that. The sole expiation that I can make is to beg your forgiveness and, should you require it, to publish openly, that is, in this journal, the admission I have just made to you."

These were my words; they were not entirely sincere, but what was sincere in them was obvious enough. My explanation had the effect upon him that I had roughly anticipated. Most old people have something deceitful, something mendacious, in their dealings with people younger than themselves; you live at peace with them, imagine you are on the best of terms with them, know their ruling prejudices, receive continual assurances of amity, take the whole thing for granted; and when something decisive happens and those peaceful relations, so long nourished, should come into effective operation, suddenly these old people rise before you like strangers, show that they have deeper and stronger convictions, and now for the first time literally unfurl their banner, and with terror you read upon it the new decree. The reason for this terror lies chiefly in the fact that what the old say now is really far more just and sensible than what they had said before; it is as if even the self-evident had degrees of validity, and their words now were more self-evident than every But the final deceit that lies in their words consists in this, that at bottom they have always said what they are saying now. I must have probed deeply into the schoolmaster, seeing that his nest words did not entirely take me by surprise. "Child," he said, laying his hand on mine and patting it gently, "how did you ever take it into your head to go into this affair? The very first I heard of it I talked it over with my wife." He pushed his chair back from the table, got up, spread out his arms, and stared at the floor, as if his tiny little wife were standing there and he were speaking to her. "'We've struggled on alone,' I said to her, 'for many years; now, it seems, a noble protector has risen for us in the city, a fine businessman, Mr. So-and-so. We should congratulate ourselves, shouldn't we? A businessman in the city isn't to be sniffed at; when an ignorant peasant believes us and says so it doesn't help us, for what a peasant may say or do is of no account; whether he says the old village schoolmaster is right, or spits to show his contempt, the net result is the same. And if instead of one peasant ten thousand should stand up for us, the result, if possible, would only be still worse. A businessman in the city, on the other hand, that's something else again; a man like that has connections, things he says in passing, as it were, are taken up and repeated, new patrons interest themselves in the question, one of them, it may be, remarks: You can learn even from old village schoolmasters, and next day whole crowds of people are saying it to one another, people you would never imagine saying such things, to look at them. Next, money is found to finance the business, one gentleman goes around collecting for it and the others shower subscriptions on him; they decide that the village schoolmaster must be dragged from his obscurity; they arrive, they don't bother about his external appearance, but take him to their bosoms, and since his wife and children hang onto him, they are taken along too. Have you ever watched city people? They chatter without stopping. When there's a whole lot of them together you can hear their chatter running from right to left and back again, and up and down, this way and that. And so, chattering away, they push us into the coach, so that we've hardly time to bow to everybody. The gentleman on the coachman's seat puts his glasses straight, flourishes his whip, and off we go. They all wave a parting greeting to the village, as if we were still there and not sitting among them. The more impatient city people drive out in carriages to meet us. As we approach they get up from their seats and crane their necks. The gentleman who collected the money arranges everything methodically and in order. When we drive into the city we are a long procession of carriages. We think the public welcome is over; but it really only begins when we reach our hotel. In a city an announcement attracts a great many people. What interests one interests all the rest immediately. They take their views from one another and promptly make those views their own. All the people who haven't managed to drive out and meet us in carriages are waiting in front of the hotel; others could have driven out, but they were too self-conscious. They're waiting too. It's extraordinary, the way that the gentleman who collected the money keeps his eye on everything and directs everything."

I had listened coolly to him, indeed I had grown cooler and cooler while he went on. On the table I had piled up all the copies of my pamphlet in my possession. Only a few were missing, for during the past week I had sent out a circular demanding the return of all the copies distributed, and had received most of them back. True, from several quarters I had got very polite notes saying that So-and-so could not remember having received such a pamphlet, and that, if it had actually arrived, he was sorry to confess that he must have lost it. Even that was gratifying; in my heart I desired nothing better. Only one reader begged me to let him keep the pamphlet as a curiosity, pledging himself, in accordance with the spirit of my circular, to show it to no one for twenty years. The village teacher had not yet seen my circular. I was glad that his words made it so easy for me to show it to him. I could do that without anxiety in any case, however, as I had drawn it up very circumspectly, keeping his interests in mind the whole time. The crucial passage in the circular ran as follows: "I do not ask for the return of the pamphlet because I retract in any way the opinions defended there or wish them to be regarded as erroneous or even undemonstrable on any point. My request has purely personal and moreover very urgent grounds; but no conclusion whatever must be drawn from it as regards my attitude to the whole matter. I beg to draw your particular attention to this, and would be glad also if you would make the fact better known."

For the time being I kept my hand over the circular and said: "You reproach me in your heart because things have not turned out as you hoped. Why do that? Don't let us embitter our last moments together. And do try to see that, though you've made a discovery, it isn't necessarily greater than every other discovery, and consequently the injustice you suffer under any greater than other injustices. I don't know the ways of learned societies, but I can't believe that in the most favorable circumstances you would have been given a reception even remotely resembling the one you seem to have described to your wife. While I myself still hoped that something might come of my pamphlet, the most I expected was that perhaps the attention of a professor might be drawn to our case, that he might commission some young student to inquire into it, that this student might visit you and check in his own fashion your and my inquiries once more on the spot, and that finally, if the results seemed to him worth consideration we must not forget that all young students are full of skepticism he might bring out a pamphlet of his own in which your discoveries would be put on a scientific basis. All the same, even if that hope had been realized nothing very much would have been achieved. The student's pamphlet, supporting such queer opinions, would probably be held up to ridicule. If you take this agricultural journal as a sample, you can see how easily that may happen; and scientific periodicals are still more ruthless in such matters. And that's quite understandable; professors bear a great responsibility toward themselves, toward science, toward posterity; they can't take every new discovery to their bosoms straight away. We others have the advantage of them there. But I'll leave that out of account and assume that the student's pamphlet has found acceptance. What would happen next? You would probably receive honorable mention, and that might perhaps benefit your profession too; people would say: 'Our village schoolmasters have sharp eyes'; and this journal, if journals have a memory or a conscience, would be forced to make you a public apology; also some well intentioned professor would be found to secure a scholarship for you; it's possible they might even get you to come to the city, find a post for you in some school, and so give you a chance of using the scientific resources of a city so as to improve yourself. But if I am to be quite frank, I think they would content themselves with merely trying to do all this. They would summon you and you would appear, but only as an ordinary petitioner like hundreds of others, and not in solemn state; they would talk to you and praise your honest efforts, but they would see at the same time that you were an old man, that it was hopeless for anyone to begin to study science at such an age, and moreover that you had hit upon your discovery more by chance than by design, and had besides no ambition to extend your labors beyond this one case. For these reasons they would probably send you back to your village again. Your discovery, of course, would be carried further, for it is not so trifling that, once having achieved recognition, it could be forgotten again. But you would not hear much more about it, and what you heard you would scarcely understand. Every new discovery is assumed at once into the sum total of knowledge, and with that ceases in a sense to be a discovery; it dissolves into the whole and disappears, and one must have a trained scientific eye even to recognize it after that. For it is related to fundamental axioms of whose existence we don't even know, and in the debates of science it is raised on these axioms into the very clouds. How can we expect to understand such things? Often as we listen to some learned discussion we may be under the impression that it is about your discovery when it is about something quite different, and the next time, when we think it is about something else, and not about your discovery at all, it may turn out to be about that and that alone.

"Don't you see that? You would remain in your village, you would be able with the extra money to feed and clothe your family a little better; but your discovery would be taken out of your hands, and without your being able with any show of justice to object; for only in the city could it be given its final seal. And people wouldn't be altogether ungrateful to you, they might build a little museum on the spot where the discovery was made, it would become one of the sights of the village, you would be given the keys to keep, and, so that you shouldn't lack some outward token of honor, they could give you a little medal to wear on the breast of your coat, like those worn by attendants in scientific institutions. All this might have been possible; but was it what you wanted?"

Without stopping to consider his answer he turned on me and said: "And so that's what you wanted to achieve for me?"

"Probably," I said, "I didn't consider what I was doing carefully enough at the time to be able to answer that clearly now. I wanted to help you, but that was a failure, and the worst failure I have ever had. That's why I want to withdraw now and undo what I've done as far as I'm able."

"Well and good," said the teacher, taking out his pipe and beginning to fill it with the tobacco that he carried loose in all his pockets. "You took up this thankless business of your own free will, and now of your own free will you withdraw. So that's all right."

"I'm not an obstinate man," I said. "Do you find anything to object to in my proposal?"

"No, absolutely nothing," said the schoolmaster, and his pipe was already going. I could not bear the stink of his tobacco, and so I rose and began to walk up and down the room. From previous encounters I was used to the teacher's extreme taciturnity, and to the fact that in spite of it he never seemed to have any desire to stir from my room once he was in it. That had often disturbed me before. He wants something more, I always thought at such times, and I would offer him money, which indeed he invariably accepted. Yet he never went away before it suited his convenience. Generally his pipe was smoked out by that time, then he would ceremoniously and respectfully push his chair in to the table, make a detour around it, seize his cane standing in the corner, press my hand warmly, and go. But today his silent presence as he sat there was an actual torture to me. When one has bidden a last farewell to someone, as I had done, a farewell accepted in good faith, surely the mutual formalities that remain should be got over as quickly as possible, and one should not burden one's host purposelessly with one's silent presence. As I contemplated the stubborn little old fellow from behind, while he sat at the table, it seemed an impossible idea ever to show him the door.

STORY 5

MOTHER SAUVAGE

Guy de Maupassant

Fifteen years had passed since I was at Virelogne. I returned there in the autumn to shoot with my friend Serval, who had at last rebuilt his chateau, which the Prussians had destroyed.

I loved that district. It is one of those delightful spots which have a sensuous charm for the eyes. You love it with a physical love. We, whom the country enchants, keep tender memories of certain springs, certain woods, certain pools, certain hills seen very often which have stirred us like joyful events. Sometimes our thoughts turn back to a corner in a forest, or the end of a bank, or an orchard filled with flowers, seen but a single time on some bright day, yet remaining in our hearts like the image of certain women met in the street on a spring morning in their light, gauzy dresses, leaving in soul and body an unsatisfied desire which is not to be forgotten, a feeling that you have just passed by happiness.

At Virelogne I loved the whole countryside, dotted with little woods and crossed by brooks which sparkled in the sun and looked like veins carrying blood to the earth. You fished in them for crawfish, trout and eels. Divine happiness! You could bathe in places and you often found snipe among the high grass which grew along the borders of these small water courses.

I was stepping along light as a goat, watching my two dogs running ahead of me, Serval, a hundred metres to my right, was beating a field of lucerne. I turned round by the thicket which forms the boundary of the wood of Sandres and I saw a cottage in ruins.

Suddenly I remembered it as I had seen it the last time, in 1869, neat, covered with vines, with chickens before the door. What is sadder than a dead house, with its skeleton standing bare and sinister?

I also recalled that inside its doors, after a very tiring day, the good woman had given me a glass of wine to drink and that Serval had told me the history of its people. The father, an old poacher, had been killed by the gendarmes. The son, whom I had once seen, was a tall, dry fellow who also passed for a fierce slayer of game. People called them "Les Sauvage."

Was that a name or a nickname?

I called to Serval. He came up with his long strides like a crane.

I asked him:

"What's become of those people?"

This was his story:

When war was declared the son Sauvage, who was then thirty-three years old, enlisted, leaving his mother alone in the house. People did not pity the old woman very much because she had money; they knew it.

She remained entirely alone in that isolated dwelling, so far from the village, on the edge of the wood. She was not afraid, however, being of the same strain as the men folk – a hardy old woman, tall and thin, who seldom laughed and with whom one never jested. The women of the fields laugh but little in any case, that is men's business. But they themselves have sad and narrowed hearts, leading a melancholy, gloomy life. The peasants imbibe a little noisy merriment at the tavern, but their helpmates always have grave, stern countenances. The muscles of their faces have never learned the motions of laughter.

Mother Sauvage continued her ordinary existence in her cottage, which was soon covered by the snows. She came to the village once a week to get bread and a little meat. Then she returned to her house. As there was talk of wolves, she went out with a gun upon her shoulder – her son's gun, rusty and with the butt worn by the rubbing of the hand – and she was a strange sight, the tall "Sauvage," a little bent, going with slow strides over the snow, the muzzle of the piece extending beyond the black headdress, which confined her head and imprisoned her white hair, which no one had ever seen.

One day a Prussian force arrived. It was billeted upon the inhabitants, according to the property and resources of each. Four were allotted to the old woman, who was known to be rich.

They were four great fellows with fair complexion, blond beards and blue eyes, who had not grown thin in spite of the fatigue which they had endured already and who also, though in a conquered country, had remained kind and gentle. Alone with this aged woman, they showed themselves full of consideration, sparing her, as much as they could, all expense and fatigue. They could be seen, all four of them, making their toilet at the well in their shirt-sleeves in the gray dawn, splashing with great swishes of water their pink-white northern skin, while La Mere Sauvage went and came, preparing their soup. They would be seen cleaning the kitchen, rubbing the tiles, splitting wood, peeling potatoes, doing up all the housework like four good sons around their mother.

But the old woman thought always of her own son, so tall and thin, with his hooked nose and his brown eyes and his heavy mustache which made a roll of black hair upon his lip. She asked every day of each of the soldiers who were installed beside her hearth: "Do you know where the French marching regiment, No. 23, was sent? My boy is in it."

They invariably answered, "No, we don't know, don't know a thing at all." And, understanding her pain and her uneasiness – they who had mothers, too, there at home – they rendered her a thousand little services. She loved them well, moreover, her four enemies, since the peasantry have no patriotic hatred; that belongs to the upper class alone. The humble, those who pay the most because they are poor and because every new burden crushes them down; those who are killed in masses, who make the true cannon's prey because they are so many; those, in fine, who suffer most cruelly the atrocious miseries of war because they are the feeblest and offer least resistance – they hardly understand at all those bellicose ardors, that excitable sense of honor or those pretended political combinations which in six months exhaust two nations, the conqueror with the conquered.

They said in the district, in speaking of the Germans of La Mere Sauvage:

"There are four who have found a soft place."

Now, one morning, when the old woman was alone in the house, she observed, far off on the plain, a man coming toward her dwelling. Soon she recognized him; it was the postman to distribute the letters. He gave her a folded paper and she drew out of her case the spectacles which she used for sewing. Then she read:

MADAME SAUVAGE: This letter is to tell you sad news. Your boy Victor was killed yesterday by a shell which almost cut him in two. I was nearby, as we stood next each other in the company, and he told me about you and asked me to let you know on the same day if anything happened to him.

I took his watch, which was in his pocket, to bring it back to you when the war is done.

Cesaire Rivot,
Soldier of the 2d class, March. Reg. No. 23.

The letter was dated three weeks back.

She did not cry at all. She remained motionless, so overcome and stupefied that she did not even suffer as yet. She thought: "There's Victor killed now." Then little by little the tears came to her eyes and the sorrow filled her heart. Her thoughts came, one by one, dreadful, torturing. She would never kiss him again, her child, her big boy, never again! The gendarmes had killed the father, the Prussians had killed the son. He had been cut in two by a cannon-ball. She seemed to see the thing, the horrible thing: the head falling, the eyes open, while he chewed the corner of his big mustache as he always did in moments of anger.

What had they done with his body afterward? If they had only let her have her boy back as they had brought back her husband – with the bullet in the middle of the forehead!

But she heard a noise of voices. It was the Prussians returning from the village. She hid her letter very quickly in her pocket, and she received them quietly, with her ordinary face, having had time to wipe her eyes.

They were laughing, all four, delighted, for they brought with them a fine rabbit – stolen, doubtless – and they made signs to the old woman that there was to be something good to east.

She set herself to work at once to prepare breakfast, but when it came to killing the rabbit, her heart failed her. And yet it was not the first. One of the soldiers struck it down with a blow of his fist behind the ears.

The beast once dead, she skinned the red body, but the sight of the blood which she was touching, and which covered her hands, and which she felt cooling and coagulating, made her tremble from head to foot, and she kept seeing her big boy cut in two, bloody, like this still palpitating animal.

She sat down at table with the Prussians, but she could not eat, not even a mouthful. They devoured the rabbit without bothering themselves about her. She looked at them sideways, without speaking, her face so impassive that they perceived nothing.

All of a sudden she said: "I don't even know your names, and here's a whole month that we've been together." They understood, not without difficulty, what she wanted, and told their names.

That was not sufficient; she had them written for her on a paper, with the addresses of their families, and, resting her spectacles on her great nose, she contemplated that strange handwriting, then folded the sheet and put it in her pocket, on top of the letter which told her of the death of her son.

When the meal was ended she said to the men:

"I am going to work for you."

And she began to carry up hay into the loft where they slept.

They were astonished at her taking all this trouble; she explained to them that thus they would not be so cold; and they helped her. They heaped the stacks of hay as high as the straw roof, and in that manner they made a sort of great chamber with four walls of fodder, warm and perfumed, where they should sleep splendidly.

At dinner one of them was worried to see that La Mere Sauvage still ate nothing. She told him that she had pains in her stomach. Then she kindled a good fire to warm herself, and the four Germans ascended to their lodging-place by the ladder which served them every night for this purpose.

As soon as they closed the trapdoor the old woman removed the ladder, then opened the outside door noiselessly and went back to look for more bundles of straw, with which she filled her kitchen. She went barefoot in the snow, so softly that no sound was heard. From time to time she listened to the sonorous and unequal snoring of the four soldiers who were fast asleep.

When she judged her preparations to be sufficient, she threw one of the bundles into the fireplace, and when it was alight she scattered it over all the others. Then she went outside again and looked.

In a few seconds the whole interior of the cottage was illumined with a brilliant light and became a frightful brasier, a gigantic fiery furnace, whose glare streamed out of the narrow window and threw a glittering beam upon the snow.

Then a great cry issued from the top of the house; it was a clamor of men shouting heartrending calls of anguish and of terror. Finally the trapdoor having given way, a whirlwind of fire shot up into the loft, pierced the straw roof, rose to the sky like the immense flame of a torch, and all the cottage flared.

Nothing more was heard therein but the crackling of the fire, the cracking of the walls, the falling of the rafters. Suddenly the roof fell in and the burning carcass of the dwelling hurled a great plume of sparks into the air, amid a cloud of smoke.

The country, all white, lit up by the fire, shone like a cloth of silver tinted with red.

A bell, far off, began to toll.

The old "Sauvage" stood before her ruined dwelling, armed with her gun, her son's gun, for fear one of those men might escape.

When she saw that it was ended, she threw her weapon into the brasier. A loud report followed.

People were coming, the peasants, the Prussians.

They found the woman seated on the trunk of a tree, calm and satisfied.

A German officer, but speaking French like a son of France, demanded:

"Where are your soldiers?"

She reached her bony arm toward the red heap of fire which was almost out and answered with a strong voice:

"There!"

They crowded round her. The Prussian asked:

"How did it take fire?"

"It was I who set it on fire."

They did not believe her, they thought that the sudden disaster had made her crazy. While all pressed round and listened, she told the story from beginning to end, from the arrival of the letter to the last shriek of the men who were burned with her house, and never omitted a detail.

When she had finished, she drew two pieces of paper from her pocket, and, in order to distinguish them by the last gleams of the fire, she again adjusted her spectacles. Then she said, showing one:

"That, that is the death of Victor." Showing the other, she added, indicating the red ruins with a bend of the head: "Here are their names, so that you can write home." She quietly held a sheet of paper out to the officer, who held her by the shoulders, and she continued:

"You must write how it happened, and you must say to their mothers that it was I who did that, Victoire Simon, la Sauvage! Do not forget."

The officer shouted some orders in German. They seized her, they threw her against the walls of her house, still hot. Then twelve men drew quickly up before her, at twenty paces. She did not move. She had understood; she waited.

An order rang out, followed instantly by a long report. A belated shot went off by itself, after the others.

The old woman did not fall. She sank as though they had cut off her legs.

The Prussian officer approached. She was almost cut in two, and in her withered hand she held her letter bathed with blood.

My friend Serval added:

"It was by way of reprisal that the Germans destroyed the chateau of the district, which belonged to me."

I thought of the mothers of those four fine fellows burned in that house and of the horrible heroism of that other mother shot against the wall.

And I picked up a little stone, still blackened by the flames.

STORY 6

THE MAGIC SHOP

HG Wells

I had seen the Magic Shop from afar several times; I had passed it once or twice, a shop window of alluring little objects, magic balls, magic hens, wonderful cones, ventriloquist dolls, the material of the basket trick, packs of cards that LOOKED all right, and all that sort of thing, but never had I thought of going in until one day, almost without warning, Gip hauled me by my finger right up to the window, and so conducted himself that there was nothing for it but to take him in. I had not thought the place was there, to tell the truth – a modest-sized frontage in Regent Street, between the picture shop and the place where the chicks run about just out of patent incubators, but there it was sure enough. I had fancied it was down nearer the Circus, or round the corner in Oxford Street, or even in Holborn; always over the way and a little inaccessible it had been, with something of the mirage in its position; but here it was now quite indisputably, and the fat end of Gip's pointing finger made a noise upon the glass.

"If I was rich," said Gip, dabbing a finger at the Disappearing Egg, "I'd buy myself that. And that" – which was The Crying Baby, Very Human – "and that," which was a mystery, and called, so a neat card asserted, "Buy One and Astonish Your Friends."

"Anything," said Gip, "will disappear under one of those cones. I have read about it in a book.

"And there, dadda, is the Vanishing Halfpenny—, only they've put it this way up so's we can't see how it's done."

Gip, dear boy, inherits his mother's breeding, and he did not propose to enter the shop or worry in any way; only, you know, quite unconsciously he lugged my finger doorward, and he made his interest clear.

"That," he said, and pointed to the Magic Bottle.

"If you had that?" I said; at which promising inquiry he looked up with a sudden radiance.

"I could show it to Jessie," he said, thoughtful as ever of others.

"It's less than a hundred days to your birthday, Gibbles," I said, and laid my hand on the door-handle.

Gip made no answer, but his grip tightened on my finger, and so we came into the shop.

It was no common shop this; it was a magic shop, and all the prancing precedence Gip would have taken in the matter of mere toys was wanting. He left the burthen of the conversation to me.

It was a little, narrow shop, not very well lit, and the door-bell pinged again with a plaintive note as we closed it behind us. For a moment or so we were alone and could glance about us. There was a tiger in papier-mache on the glass case that covered the low counter – a grave, kind-eyed tiger that waggled his head in a methodical manner; there were several crystal spheres, a china hand holding magic cards, a stock of magic fish-bowls in various sizes, and an immodest magic hat that shamelessly displayed its springs. On the floor were magic mirrors; one to draw you out long and thin, one to swell your head and vanish your legs, and one to make you short and fat like a draught; and while we were laughing at these the shopman, as I suppose, came in.

At any rate, there he was behind the counter – a curious, sallow, dark man, with one ear larger than the other and a chin like the toe-cap of a boot.

"What can we have the pleasure?" he said, spreading his long, magic fingers on the glass case; and so with a start we were aware of him.

"I want," I said, "to buy my little boy a few simple tricks."

"Legerdemain?" he asked. "Mechanical? Domestic?"

"Anything amusing?" said I.

"Um!" said the shopman, and scratched his head for a moment as if thinking. Then, quite distinctly, he drew from his head a glass ball. "Something in this way?" he said, and held it out.

The action was unexpected. I had seen the trick done at entertainments endless times before – it's part of the common stock of conjurers – but I had not expected it here.

"That's good," I said, with a laugh.

"Isn't it?" said the shopman.

Gip stretched out his disengaged hand to take this object and found merely a blank palm.

"It's in your pocket," said the shopman, and there it was!

"How much will that be?" I asked.

"We make no charge for glass balls," said the shopman politely. "We get them," – he picked one out of his elbow as he spoke – "free." He produced another from the back of his neck, and laid it beside its predecessor on the counter. Gip regarded his glass ball sagely, then directed a look of inquiry at the two on the counter, and finally brought his round-eyed scrutiny to the shopman, who smiled.

"You may have those too," said the shopman, "and, if you DON'T mind, one from my mouth. SO!"

Gip counselled me mutely for a moment, and then in a profound silence put away the four balls, resumed my reassuring finger, and nerved himself for the next event.

"We get all our smaller tricks in that way," the shopman remarked.

I laughed in the manner of one who subscribes to a jest. "Instead of going to the wholesale shop," I said. "Of course, it's cheaper."

"In a way," the shopman said. "Though we pay in the end. But not so heavily – as people suppose.... Our larger tricks, and our daily provisions and all the other things we want, we get out of that hat... And you know, sir, if you'll excuse my saying it, there ISN'T a wholesale shop, not for Genuine Magic goods, sir. I don't know if you noticed our inscription – the Genuine Magic shop." He drew a business-card from his cheek and handed it to me. "Genuine," he said, with his finger on the word, and added, "There is absolutely no deception, sir."

He seemed to be carrying out the joke pretty thoroughly, I thought.

He turned to Gip with a smile of remarkable affability. "You, you know, are the Right Sort of Boy."

I was surprised at his knowing that, because, in the interests of discipline, we keep it rather a secret even at home; but Gip received it in unflinching silence, keeping a steadfast eye on him.

"It's only the Right Sort of Boy gets through that doorway."

And, as if by way of illustration, there came a rattling at the door, and a squeaking little voice could be faintly heard. "Nyar! I WARN 'a go in there, dadda, I WARN 'a go in there. Ny-a-a-ah!" and then the accents of a down-trodden parent, urging consolations and propitiations. "It's locked, Edward," he said.

"But it isn't," said I.

"It is, sir," said the shopman, "always – for that sort of child," and as he spoke we had a glimpse of the other youngster, a little, white face, pallid from sweet-eating and over-sapid food, and distorted by evil passions, a ruthless little egotist, pawing at the enchanted pane. "It's no good, sir," said the shopman, as I moved, with my natural helpfulness, doorward, and presently the spoilt child was carried off howling.

"How do you manage that?" I said, breathing a little more freely.

"Magic!" said the shopman, with a careless wave of the hand, and behold! sparks of coloured fire flew out of his fingers and vanished into the shadows of the shop.

"You were saying," he said, addressing himself to Gip, "before you came in, that you would like one of our 'Buy One and Astonish your Friends' boxes?"

Gip, after a gallant effort, said "Yes."

"It's in your pocket."

And leaning over the counter – he really had an extraordinarily long body – this amazing person produced the article in the customary conjurer's manner. "Paper," he said, and took a sheet out of the empty hat with the springs; "string," and behold his mouth was a string-box, from which he drew an unending thread, which when he had tied his parcel he bit off – and, it seemed to me, swallowed the ball of string. And then he lit a candle at the nose of one of the ventriloquist's dummies, stuck one of his fingers (which had become sealing-wax red) into the flame, and so sealed the parcel. "Then there was the Disappearing Egg," he remarked, and produced one from within my coat-breast and packed it, and also The Crying Baby, Very Human. I handed each parcel to Gip as it was ready, and he clasped them to his chest.

He said very little, but his eyes were eloquent; the clutch of his arms was eloquent. He was the playground of unspeakable emotions. These, you know, were REAL Magics. Then, with a start, I discovered something moving about in my hat – something soft and jumpy. I whipped it off, and a ruffled pigeon – no doubt a confederate – dropped out and ran on the counter, and went, I fancy, into a cardboard box behind the papier-mâché tiger.

"Tut, tut!" said the shopman, dexterously relieving me of my headdress; "careless bird, and – as I live – nesting!"

He shook my hat, and shook out into his extended hand two or three eggs, a large marble, a watch, about half-a-dozen of the inevitable glass balls, and then crumpled, crinkled paper, more and more and more, talking all the time of the way in which people neglect to brush their hats INSIDE as well as out, politely, of course, but with a certain personal application. "All sorts of things accumulate, sir.... Not YOU, of course, in particular.... Nearly every customer.... Astonishing what they carry about with them...." The crumpled paper rose and billowed on the counter more and more and more, until he was nearly hidden from us, until he was altogether hidden, and still his voice went on and on. "We none of us know what the fair semblance of a human being may conceal, sir. Are we all then no better than brushed exteriors, whited sepulchres—"

His voice stopped – exactly like when you hit a neighbour's gramophone with a well-aimed brick, the same instant silence, and the rustle of the paper stopped, and everything was still....

"Have you done with my hat?" I said, after an interval.

There was no answer.

I stared at Gip, and Gip stared at me, and there were our distortions in the magic mirrors, looking very rum, and grave, and quiet....

"I think we'll go now," I said. "Will you tell me how much all this comes to?....

"I say," I said, on a rather louder note, "I want the bill; and my hat, please."

It might have been a sniff from behind the paper pile....

"Let's look behind the counter, Gip," I said. "He's making fun of us."

I led Gip round the head-wagging tiger, and what do you think there was behind the counter? No one at all! Only my hat on the floor, and a common conjurer's lop-eared white rabbit lost in meditation, and looking as stupid and crumpled as only a conjurer's rabbit can do. I resumed my hat, and the rabbit lolloped a lollop or so out of my way.

"Dadda!" said Gip, in a guilty whisper.

"What is it, Gip?" said I.

"I DO like this shop, dadda."

"So should I," I said to myself, "if the counter wouldn't suddenly extend itself to shut one off from the door." But I didn't call Gip's attention to that. "Pussy!" he said, with a hand out to the rabbit as it came lolloping past us; "Pussy, do Gip a magic!" and his eyes followed it as it squeezed through a door I had certainly not remarked a moment before. Then this door opened wider, and the man with one ear larger than the other appeared again. He was smiling still, but his eye met mine with something between amusement and defiance. "You'd like to see our show-room, sir," he said, with an innocent suavity. Gip tugged my finger forward. I glanced at the counter and met the shopman's eye again. I was beginning to think the magic just a little too genuine. "We haven't VERY much time," I said. But somehow we were inside the show-room before I could finish that.

"All goods of the same quality," said the shopman, rubbing his flexible hands together, "and that is the Best. Nothing in the place that isn't genuine Magic, and warranted thoroughly rum. Excuse me, sir!"

I felt him pull at something that clung to my coat-sleeve, and then I saw he held a little, wriggling red demon by the tail – the little creature bit and fought and tried to get at his hand – and in a moment he tossed it carelessly behind a counter. No doubt the thing was only an image of twisted indiarubber, but for the moment—! And his gesture was exactly that of a man who handles some petty biting bit of vermin. I glanced at Gip, but Gip was looking at a magic rocking-horse. I was glad he hadn't seen the thing. "I say," I said, in an undertone, and indicating Gip and the red demon with my eyes, "you haven't many things like THAT about, have you?"

"None of ours! Probably brought it with you," said the shopman – also in an undertone, and with a more dazzling smile than ever. "Astonishing what people WILL carry about with them unawares!" And then to Gip, "Do you see anything you fancy here?"

There were many things that Gip fancied there.

He turned to this astonishing tradesman with mingled confidence and respect. "Is that a Magic Sword?" he said.

"A Magic Toy Sword. It neither bends, breaks, nor cuts the fingers. It renders the bearer invincible in battle against anyone under eighteen. Half-a-crown to seven and sixpence, according to size. These panoplies on cards are for juvenile knights-errant and very useful – shield of safety, sandals of swiftness, helmet of invisibility."

"Oh, daddy!" gasped Gip.

I tried to find out what they cost, but the shopman did not heed me. He had got Gip now; he had got him away from my finger; he had embarked upon the exposition of all his confounded stock, and nothing was going to stop him. Presently I saw with a qualm of distrust and something very like jealousy that Gip had hold of this person's finger as usually he has hold of mine. No doubt the fellow was interesting, I thought, and had an interestingly faked lot of stuff, really GOOD faked stuff, still—

I wandered after them, saying very little, but keeping an eye on this prestidigital fellow. After all, Gip was enjoying it. And no doubt when the time came to go we should be able to go quite easily.

It was a long, rambling place, that show-room, a gallery broken up by stands and stalls and pillars, with archways leading off to other departments, in which the queerest-looking assistants loafed and stared at one, and with perplexing mirrors and curtains. So perplexing, indeed, were these that I was presently unable to make out the door by which we had come.

The shopman showed Gip magic trains that ran without steam or clockwork, just as you set the signals, and then some very, very valuable boxes of soldiers that all came alive directly you took off the lid and said—. I myself haven't a very quick ear and it was a tongue-twisting sound, but Gip – he has his mother's ear – got it in no time. "Bravo!" said the shopman, putting the men back into the box unceremoniously and handing it to Gip. "Now," said the shopman, and in a moment Gip had made them all alive again.

"You'll take that box?" asked the shopman.

"We'll take that box," said I, "unless you charge its full value. In which case it would need a Trust Magnate—"

"Dear heart! NO!" and the shopman swept the little men back again, shut the lid, waved the box in the air, and there it was, in brown paper, tied up and – WITH GIP'S FULL NAME AND ADDRESS ON THE PAPER!

The shopman laughed at my amazement.

"This is the genuine magic," he said. "The real thing."

"It's a little too genuine for my taste," I said again.

After that he fell to showing Gip tricks, odd tricks, and still odder the way they were done. He explained them, he turned them inside out, and there was the dear little chap nodding his busy bit of a head in the sagest manner.

I did not attend as well as I might. "Hey, presto!" said the Magic Shopman, and then would come the clear, small "Hey, presto!"

of the boy. But I was distracted by other things. It was being borne in upon me just how tremendously rum this place was; it was, so to speak, inundated by a sense of rumness. There was something a little rum about the fixtures even, about the ceiling, about the floor, about the casually distributed chairs. I had a queer feeling that whenever I wasn't looking at them straight they went askew, and moved about, and played a noiseless puss-in-the-corner behind my back. And the cornice had a serpentine design with masks – masks altogether too expressive for proper plaster.

Then abruptly my attention was caught by one of the odd-looking assistants. He was some way off and evidently unaware of my presence – I saw a sort of three-quarter length of him over a pile of toys and through an arch – and, you know, he was leaning against a pillar in an idle sort of way doing the most horrid things with his features! The particular horrid thing he did was with his nose. He did it just as though he was idle and wanted to amuse himself. First of all it was a short, blobby nose, and then suddenly he shot it out like a telescope, and then out it flew and became thinner and thinner until it was like a long, red, flexible whip. Like a thing in a nightmare it was! He flourished it about and flung it forth as a fly-fisher flings his line.

My instant thought was that Gip mustn't see him. I turned about, and there was Gip quite preoccupied with the shopman, and thinking no evil. They were whispering together and looking at me. Gip was standing on a little stool, and the shopman was holding a sort of big drum in his hand.

"Hide and seek, dadda!" cried Gip. "You're He!"

And before I could do anything to prevent it, the shopman had clapped the big drum over him. I saw what was up directly. "Take that off," I cried, "this instant! You'll frighten the boy. Take it off!"

The shopman with the unequal ears did so without a word, and held the big cylinder towards me to show its emptiness. And the little stool was vacant! In that instant my boy had utterly disappeared?...

You know, perhaps, that sinister something that comes like a hand out of the unseen and grips your heart about. You know it takes your common self away and leaves you tense and deliberate, neither slow nor hasty, neither angry nor afraid. So it was with me.

I came up to this grinning shopman and kicked his stool aside.

"Stop this folly!" I said. "Where is my boy?"

"You see," he said, still displaying the drum's interior, "there is no deception—"

I put out my hand to grip him, and he eluded me by a dexterous movement. I snatched again, and he turned from me and pushed open a door to escape. "Stop!" I said, and he laughed, receding. I leapt after him – into utter darkness.

THUD!

"Lor' bless my 'eart! I didn't see you coming, sir!"

I was in Regent Street, and I had collided with a decent-looking working man; and a yard away, perhaps, and looking a little perplexed with himself, was Gip. There was some sort of apology, and then Gip had turned and come to me with a bright little smile, as though for a moment he had missed me.

And he was carrying four parcels in his arm!

He secured immediate possession of my finger.

For the second I was rather at a loss. I stared round to see the door of the magic shop, and, behold, it was not there! There was no door, no shop, nothing, only the common pilaster between the shop where they sell pictures and the window with the chicks!...

I did the only thing possible in that mental tumult; I walked straight to the kerbstone and held up my umbrella for a cab.

"'Ansoms," said Gip, in a note of culminating exultation.

I helped him in, recalled my address with an effort, and got in also. Something unusual proclaimed itself in my tail-coat pocket, and I felt and discovered a glass ball. With a petulant expression I flung it into the street.

Gip said nothing.

For a space neither of us spoke.

"Dada!" said Gip, at last, "that WAS a proper shop!"

I came round with that to the problem of just how the whole thing had seemed to him. He looked completely undamaged – so far, good; he was neither scared nor unhinged, he was simply tremendously satisfied with the afternoon's entertainment, and there in his arms were the four parcels.

Confound it! What could be in them?

"Um!" I said. "Little boys can't go to shops like that every day."

He received this with his usual stoicism, and for a moment I was sorry I was his father and not his mother, and so couldn't suddenly there, coram publico, in our hansom, kiss him. After all, I thought, the thing wasn't so very bad.

But it was only when we opened the parcels that I really began to be reassured. Three of them contained boxes of soldiers, quite ordinary lead soldiers, but of so good a quality as to make Gip altogether forget that originally these parcels had been Magic Tricks of the only genuine sort, and the fourth contained a kitten, a little living white kitten, in excellent health and appetite and temper.

I saw this unpacking with a sort of provisional relief. I hung about in the nursery for quite an unconscionable time....

That happened six months ago. And now I am beginning to believe it is all right. The kitten had only the magic natural to all kittens, and the soldiers seem as steady a company as any colonel could desire. And Gip—?

The intelligent parent will understand that I have to go cautiously with Gip.

But I went so far as this one day. I said, "How would you like your soldiers to come alive, Gip, and march about by themselves?"

"Mine do," said Gip. "I just have to say a word I know before I open the lid."

"Then they march about alone?"

"Oh, QUITE, dadda. I shouldn't like them if they didn't do that."

I displayed no unbecoming surprise, and since then I have taken occasion to drop in upon him once or twice, unannounced, when the soldiers were about, but so far I have never discovered them performing in anything like a magical manner.

It's so difficult to tell.

There's also a question of finance. I have an incurable habit of paying bills. I have been up and down Regent Street several times, looking for that shop. I am inclined to think, indeed, that in that matter honour is satisfied, and that, since Gip's name and address are known to them, I may very well leave it to these people, whoever they may be, to send in their bill in their own time.

STORY 7

A LITERARY NIGHTMARE

Mark Twain

Will the reader please to cast his eye over the following lines, and see if he can discover anything harmful in them?

> *Conductor, when you receive a fare,*
> *Punch in the presence of the passenjare!*
> *A blue trip slip for an eight-cent fare,*
> *A buff trip slip for a six-cent fare,*
> *A pink trip slip for a three-cent fare,*
> *Punch in the presence of the passenjare!*
>
> CHORUS
>
> *Punch, brothers! punch with care!*
> *Punch in the presence of the passenjare!*

I came across these jingling rhymes in a newspaper, a little while ago, and read them a couple of times. They took instant and entire possession of me. All through breakfast they went waltzing through my brain; and when, at last, I rolled up my napkin,

I could not tell whether I had eaten anything or not. I had carefully laid out my day's work the day before – thrilling tragedy in the novel which I am writing. I went to my den to begin my deed of blood. I took up my pen, but all I could get it to say was, "Punch in the presence of the passenjare." I fought hard for an hour, but it was useless. My head kept humming, "A blue trip slip for an eight-cent fare, a buff trip slip for a six-cent fare," and so on and so on, without peace or respite. The day's work was ruined – I could see that plainly enough. I gave up and drifted down-town, and presently discovered that my feet were keeping time to that relentless jingle.

When I could stand it no longer I altered my step. But it did no good; those rhymes accommodated themselves to the new step and went on harassing me just as before. I returned home, and suffered all the afternoon; suffered all through an unconscious and unrefreshing dinner; suffered, and cried, and jingled all through the evening; went to bed and rolled, tossed, and jingled right along, the same as ever; got up at midnight frantic, and tried to read; but there was nothing visible upon the whirling page except "Punch! punch in the presence of the passenjare." By sunrise I was out of my mind, and everybody marveled and was distressed at the idiotic burden of my ravings – "Punch! oh, punch! punch in the presence of the passenjare!"

Two days later, on Saturday morning, I arose, a tottering wreck, and went forth to fulfil an engagement with a valued friend, the Rev. Mr. ———, to walk to the Talcott Tower, ten miles distant. He stared at me, but asked no questions. We started. Mr. ——— talked, talked, talked as is his wont. I said nothing; I heard nothing. At the end of a mile, Mr. ——— said "Mark, are you sick? I never saw a man look so haggard and worn and absent-minded. Say something, do!"

Drearily, without enthusiasm, I said: "Punch brothers, punch with care! Punch in the presence of the passenjare!"

My friend eyed me blankly, looked perplexed, they said:

"I do not think I get your drift, Mark. Then does not seem to be any relevancy in what you have said, certainly nothing sad; and yet – maybe it was the way you said the words – I never heard anything that sounded so pathetic. What is—"

But I heard no more. I was already far away with my pitiless, heartbreaking "blue trip slip for an eight-cent fare, buff trip slip for a six-cent fare, pink trip slip for a three-cent fare; punch in the presence of the passenjare." I do not know what occurred during the other nine miles. However, all of a sudden Mr. ——— laid his hand on my shoulder and shouted:

"Oh, wake up! Wake up! Wake up! Don't sleep all day! Here we are at the Tower, man! I have talked myself deaf and dumb and blind, and never got a response. Just look at this magnificent autumn landscape! Look at it! Look at it! Feast your eye on it! You have traveled; you have seen boaster landscapes elsewhere. Come, now, deliver an honest opinion. What do you say to this?"

I sighed wearily; and murmured:

"A buff trip slip for a six-cent fare, a pink trip slip for a three-cent fare, punch in the presence of the passenjare."

Rev. Mr. ——— stood there, very grave, full of concern, apparently, and looked long at me; then he said:

"Mark, there is something about this that I cannot understand. Those are about the same words you said before; there does not seem to be anything in them, and yet they nearly break my heart when you say them. Punch in the – how is it they go?"

I began at the beginning and repeated all the lines.

My friend's face lighted with interest. He said:

"Why, what a captivating jingle it is! It is almost music. It flows along so nicely. I have nearly caught the rhymes myself. Say them over just once more, and then I'll have them, sure."

I said them over. Then Mr. —————— said them. He made one little mistake, which I corrected. The next time and the next he got them right. Now a great burden seemed to tumble from my shoulders. That torturing jingle departed out of my brain, and a grateful sense of rest and peace descended upon me. I was light-hearted enough to sing; and I did sing for half an hour, straight along, as we went jogging homeward. Then my freed tongue found blessed speech again, and the pent talk of many a weary hour began to gush and flow. It flowed on and on, joyously, jubilantly, until the fountain was empty and dry. As I wrung my friend's hand at parting, I said:

"Haven't we had a royal good time! But now I remember, you haven't said a word for two hours. Come, come, out with something!"

The Rev. Mr. —————— turned a lack-luster eye upon me, drew a deep sigh, and said, without animation, without apparent consciousness:

"Punch, brothers, punch with care! Punch in the presence of the passenjare!"

A pang shot through me as I said to myself, "Poor fellow, poor fellow! he has got it, now."

I did not see Mr. —————— for two or three days after that. Then, on Tuesday evening, he staggered into my presence and sank dejectedly into a seat. He was pale, worn; he was a wreck. He lifted his faded eyes to my face and said:

"Ah, Mark, it was a ruinous investment that I made in those heartless rhymes. They have ridden me like a nightmare, day and night, hour after hour, to this very moment. Since I saw you

I have suffered the torments of the lost. Saturday evening I had a sudden call, by telegraph, and took the night train for Boston. The occasion was the death of a valued old friend who had requested that I should preach his funeral sermon. I took my seat in the cars and set myself to framing the discourse. But I never got beyond the opening paragraph; for then the train started and the car-wheels began their 'clack, clack-clack-clack-clack! clack-clack! clack-clack-clack!' and right away those odious rhymes fitted themselves to that accompaniment. For an hour I sat there and set a syllable of those rhymes to every separate and distinct clack the car-wheels made. Why, I was as fagged out, then, as if I had been chopping wood all day. My skull was splitting with headache. It seemed to me that I must go mad if I sat there any longer; so I undressed and went to bed. I stretched myself out in my berth, and – well, you know what the result was. The thing went right along, just the same. 'Clack-clack clack, a blue trip slip, clack-clack-clack, for an eight cent fare; clack-clack-clack, a buff trip slip, clack clack-clack, for a six-cent fare, and so on, and so on, and so on punch in the presence of the passenjare!' Sleep? Not a single wink! I was almost a lunatic when I got to Boston. Don't ask me about the funeral. I did the best I could, but every solemn individual sentence was meshed and tangled and woven in and out with 'Punch, brothers, punch with care, punch in the presence of the passenjare.' And the most distressing thing was that my delivery dropped into the undulating rhythm of those pulsing rhymes, and I could actually catch absent-minded people nodding time to the swing of it with their stupid heads. And, Mark, you may believe it or not, but before I got through the entire assemblage were placidly bobbing their heads in solemn unison, mourners, undertaker, and all. The moment I had finished, I fled to the anteroom in a state bordering on frenzy. Of course it would be my luck to find a sorrowing and aged maiden aunt of the deceased there, who had arrived from Springfield too late to get into the church. She began to sob, and said:

"'Oh, oh, he is gone, he is gone, and I didn't see him before he died!'

"'Yes!' I said, 'he is gone, he is gone, he is gone – oh, will this suffering never cease!'

"'You loved him, then! Oh, you too loved him!'

"'Loved him! Loved who?'

"'Why, my poor George! my poor nephew!'

"'Oh – him! Yes – oh, yes, yes. Certainly – certainly. Punch – punch – oh, this misery will kill me!'

"'Bless you! Bless you, sir, for these sweet words! I, too, suffer in this dear loss. Were you present during his last moments?'

"'Yes. I – whose last moments?'

"'His. The dear departed's.'

"'Yes! Oh, yes – yes – yes! I suppose so, I think so, I don't know! Oh, certainly – I was there I was there!'

"'Oh, what a privilege! What a precious privilege! And his last words – oh, tell me, tell me his last words! What did he say?'

"'He said – he said – oh, my head, my head, my head! He said – he said – he never said anything but Punch, punch, punch in the presence of the passenjare! Oh, leave me, madam! In the name of all that is generous, leave me to my madness, my misery, my despair! – a buff trip slip for a six-cent fare, a pink trip slip for a three-cent fare – endurance can no further go! – PUNCH in the presence of the passenjare!"

My friend's hopeless eyes rested upon mine a pregnant minute, and then he said impressively:

"Mark, you do not say anything. You do not offer me any hope. But, ah me, it is just as well – it is just as well. You could not do me any good. The time has long gone by when words could comfort me. Something tells me that my tongue is doomed to wag forever to the jigger of that remorseless jingle. There – there it is coming on me again: a blue trip slip for an eight-cent fare, a buff trip slip for a—"

Thus murmuring faint and fainter, my friend sank into a peaceful trance and forgot his sufferings in a blessed respite.

How did I finally save him from an asylum? I took him to a neighboring university and made him discharge the burden of his persecuting rhymes into the eager ears of the poor, unthinking students. How is it with them, now? The result is too sad to tell. Why did I write this article? It was for a worthy, even a noble, purpose. It was to warn you, reader, if you should came across those merciless rhymes, to avoid them – avoid them as you would a pestilence.

STORY 8

AFTER TWENTY YEARS

O Henry

The policeman on the beat moved up the avenue impressively. The impressiveness was habitual and not for show, for spectators were few. The time was barely 10 o'clock at night, but chilly gusts of wind with a taste of rain in them had well nigh de-peopled the streets.

Trying doors as he went, twirling his club with many intricate and artful movements, turning now and then to cast his watchful eye adown the pacific thoroughfare, the officer, with his stalwart form and slight swagger, made a fine picture of a guardian of the peace. The vicinity was one that kept early hours. Now and then you might see the lights of a cigar store or of an all-night lunch counter; but the majority of the doors belonged to business places that had long since been closed.

When about midway of a certain block the policeman suddenly slowed his walk. In the doorway of a darkened hardware store a man leaned, with an unlighted cigar in his mouth. As the policeman walked up to him the man spoke up quickly.

"It's all right, officer," he said, reassuringly. "I'm just waiting for a friend. It's an appointment made twenty years ago. Sounds a little funny to you, doesn't it? Well, I'll explain if you'd like to make certain it's all straight. About that long ago there used to be a restaurant where this store stands – 'Big Joe' Brady's restaurant."

"Until five years ago," said the policeman. "It was torn down then."

The man in the doorway struck a match and lit his cigar. The light showed a pale, square-jawed face with keen eyes, and a little white scar near his right eyebrow. His scarfpin was a large diamond, oddly set.

"Twenty years ago to-night," said the man, "I dined here at 'Big Joe' Brady's with Jimmy Wells, my best chum, and the finest chap in the world. He and I were raised here in New York, just like two brothers, together. I was eighteen and Jimmy was twenty. The next morning I was to start for the West to make my fortune. You couldn't have dragged Jimmy out of New York; he thought it was the only place on earth. Well, we agreed that night that we would meet here again exactly twenty years from that date and time, no matter what our conditions might be or from what distance we might have to come. We figured that in twenty years each of us ought to have our destiny worked out and our fortunes made, whatever they were going to be."

"It sounds pretty interesting," said the policeman. "Rather a long time between meets, though, it seems to me. Haven't you heard from your friend since you left?"

"Well, yes, for a time we corresponded," said the other. "But after a year or two we lost track of each other. You see, the West is a pretty big proposition, and I kept hustling around over it pretty lively. But I know Jimmy will meet me here if he's alive, for he always was the truest, stanchest old chap in the world. He'll never forget. I came a thousand miles to stand in this door to-night, and it's worth it if my old partner turns up."

The waiting man pulled out a handsome watch, the lids of it set with small diamonds.

"Three minutes to ten," he announced. "It was exactly ten o'clock when we parted here at the restaurant door."

"Did pretty well out West, didn't you?" asked the policeman.

"You bet! I hope Jimmy has done half as well. He was a kind of plodder, though, good fellow as he was. I've had to compete with some of the sharpest wits going to get my pile. A man gets in a groove in New York. It takes the West to put a razor-edge on him."

The policeman twirled his club and took a step or two.

"I'll be on my way. Hope your friend comes around all right. Going to call time on him sharp?"

"I should say not!" said the other. "I'll give him half an hour at least. If Jimmy is alive on earth he'll be here by that time. So long, officer."

"Good-night, sir," said the policeman, passing on along his beat, trying doors as he went.

There was now a fine, cold drizzle falling, and the wind had risen from its uncertain puffs into a steady blow. The few foot passengers astir in that quarter hurried dismally and silently along with coat collars turned high and pocketed hands. And in the door of the hardware store the man who had come a thousand miles to fill an appointment, uncertain almost to absurdity, with the friend of his youth, smoked his cigar and waited.

About twenty minutes he waited, and then a tall man in a long overcoat, with collar turned up to his ears, hurried across from the opposite side of the street. He went directly to the waiting man.

"Is that you, Bob?" he asked, doubtfully.

"Is that you, Jimmy Wells?" cried the man in the door.

"Bless my heart!" exclaimed the new arrival, grasping both the other's hands with his own. "It's Bob, sure as fate. I was certain I'd find you here if you were still in existence. Well, well, well! — twenty years is a long time. The old restaurant's gone, Bob; I wish it had lasted, so we could have had another dinner there. How has the West treated you, old man?"

"Bully; it has given me everything I asked it for. You've changed lots, Jimmy. I never thought you were so tall by two or three inches."

"Oh, I grew a bit after I was twenty."

"Doing well in New York, Jimmy?"

"Moderately. I have a position in one of the city departments. Come on, Bob; we'll go around to a place I know of, and have a good long talk about old times."

The two men started up the street, arm in arm. The man from the West, his egotism enlarged by success, was beginning to outline the history of his career. The other, submerged in his overcoat, listened with interest.

At the corner stood a drug store, brilliant with electric lights. When they came into this glare each of them turned simultaneously to gaze upon the other's face.

The man from the West stopped suddenly and released his arm.

"You're not Jimmy Wells," he snapped. "Twenty years is a long time, but not long enough to change a man's nose from a Roman to a pug."

"It sometimes changes a good man into a bad one," said the tall man. "You've been under arrest for ten minutes, 'Silky' Bob. Chicago thinks you may have dropped over our way and wires us she wants to have a chat with you. Going quietly, are you? That's sensible. Now, before we go on to the station here's a note I was asked to hand you. You may read it here at the window. It's from Patrolman Wells."

The man from the West unfolded the little piece of paper handed him. His hand was steady when he began to read, but it trembled a little by the time he had finished. The note was rather short.

Bob: I was at the appointed place on time. When you struck the match to light your cigar I saw it was the face of the man wanted in Chicago. Somehow I couldn't do it myself, so I went around and got a plain clothes man to do the job.

JIMMY

STORY 9

THE LUMBER ROOM

Saki

The children were to be driven, as a special treat, to the sands at Jagborough. Nicholas was not to be of the party; he was in disgrace. Only that morning he had refused to eat his wholesome bread-and-milk on the seemingly frivolous ground that there was a frog in it. Older and wiser and better people had told him that there could not possibly be a frog in his bread-and-milk and that he was not to talk nonsense; he continued, nevertheless, to talk what seemed the veriest nonsense, and described with much detail the colouration and markings of the alleged frog. The dramatic part of the incident was that there really was a frog in Nicholas' basin of bread-and-milk; he had put it there himself, so he felt entitled to know something about it. The sin of taking a frog from the garden and putting it into a bowl of wholesome bread-and-milk was enlarged on at great length, but the fact that stood out clearest in the whole affair, as it presented itself to the mind of Nicholas, was that the older, wiser, and better people had been proved to be profoundly in error in matters about which they had expressed the utmost assurance.

"You said there couldn't possibly be a frog in my bread-and-milk; there *was* a frog in my bread-and-milk," he repeated, with the insistence of a skilled tactician who does not intend to shift from favourable ground.

So his boy-cousin and girl-cousin and his quite uninteresting younger brother were to be taken to Jagborough sands that afternoon and he was to stay at home. His cousins' aunt, who insisted, by an unwarranted stretch of imagination, in styling herself his aunt also, had hastily invented the Jagborough expedition in order to impress on Nicholas the delights that he had justly forfeited by his disgraceful conduct at the breakfast-table. It was her habit, whenever one of the children fell from grace, to improvise something of a festival nature from which the offender would be rigorously debarred; if all the children sinned collectively they were suddenly informed of a circus in a neighbouring town, a circus of unrivalled merit and uncounted elephants, to which, but for their depravity, they would have been taken that very day.

A few decent tears were looked for on the part of Nicholas when the moment for the departure of the expedition arrived. As a matter of fact, however, all the crying was done by his girl-cousin, who scraped her knee rather painfully against the step of the carriage as she was scrambling in.

"How she did howl," said Nicholas cheerfully, as the party drove off without any of the elation of high spirits that should have characterised it.

"She'll soon get over that," said the *soi-disant* aunt; "it will be a glorious afternoon for racing about over those beautiful sands. How they will enjoy themselves!"

"Bobby won't enjoy himself much, and he won't race much either," said Nicholas with a grim chuckle; "his boots are hurting him. They're too tight."

"Why didn't he tell me they were hurting?" asked the aunt with some asperity.

"He told you twice, but you weren't listening. You often don't listen when we tell you important things."

"You are not to go into the gooseberry garden," said the aunt, changing the subject.

"Why not?" demanded Nicholas.

"Because you are in disgrace," said the aunt loftily.

Nicholas did not admit the flawlessness of the reasoning; he felt perfectly capable of being in disgrace and in a gooseberry garden at the same moment. His face took on an expression of considerable obstinacy. It was clear to his aunt that he was determined to get into the gooseberry garden, "only," as she remarked to herself, "because I have told him he is not to."

Now the gooseberry garden had two doors by which it might be entered, and once a small person like Nicholas could slip in there he could effectually disappear from view amid the masking growth of artichokes, raspberry canes, and fruit bushes. The aunt had many other things to do that afternoon, but she spent an hour or two in trivial gardening operations among flower beds and shrubberies, whence she could keep a watchful eye on the two doors that led to the forbidden paradise. She was a woman of few ideas, with immense powers of concentration.

Nicholas made one or two sorties into the front garden, wriggling his way with obvious stealth of purpose towards one or other of the doors, but never able for a moment to evade the aunt's watchful eye. As a matter of fact, he had no intention of trying to get into the gooseberry garden, but it was extremely convenient for him that his aunt should believe that he had; it was a belief that would keep her on self-imposed sentry-duty for the greater part of the afternoon. Having thoroughly confirmed and fortified her suspicions Nicholas slipped back into the house and rapidly put into execution a plan of action that had long germinated in his brain. By standing on a chair in the library one could reach a shelf on which reposed a fat, important-looking key. The key was as important as it looked; it was the instrument which kept the mysteries of the lumber-room secure from unauthorised intrusion, which opened a way only for aunts and such-like privileged persons. Nicholas had not had much experience of the art of fitting keys into keyholes and turning locks, but for some days past he had practised with the key of the schoolroom door; he did not believe in trusting too much to luck and accident. The key turned stiffly in the lock, but it turned. The door opened, and Nicholas was in an unknown land, compared with which the gooseberry garden was a stale delight, a mere material pleasure.

Often and often Nicholas had pictured to himself what the lumber-room might be like, that region that was so carefully sealed from youthful eyes and concerning which no questions were ever answered. It came up to his expectations. In the first place it was large and dimly lit, one high window opening on to the forbidden garden being its only source of illumination. In the second place it was a storehouse of unimagined treasures. The aunt-by-assertion was one of those people who think that things spoil by use and consign them to dust and damp by way of preserving them. Such parts of the house as Nicholas knew best were rather bare and cheerless, but here there were wonderful things for the eye to feast on. First and foremost there was a piece of framed tapestry that was evidently meant to be a fire-screen.

To Nicholas it was a living, breathing story; he sat down on a roll of Indian hangings, glowing in wonderful colours beneath a layer of dust, and took in all the details of the tapestry picture. A man, dressed in the hunting costume of some remote period, had just transfixed a stag with an arrow; it could not have been a difficult shot because the stag was only one or two paces away from him; in the thickly-growing vegetation that the picture suggested it would not have been difficult to creep up to a feeding stag, and the two spotted dogs that were springing forward to join in the chase had evidently been trained to keep to heel till the arrow was discharged. That part of the picture was simple, if interesting, but did the huntsman see, what Nicholas saw, that four galloping wolves were coming in his direction through the wood? There might be more than four of them hidden behind the trees, and in any case would the man and his dogs be able to cope with the four wolves if they made an attack? The man had only two arrows left in his quiver, and he might miss with one or both of them; all one knew about his skill in shooting was that he could hit a large stag at a ridiculously short range. Nicholas sat for many golden minutes revolving the possibilities of the scene; he was inclined to think that there were more than four wolves and that the man and his dogs were in a tight corner.

But there were other objects of delight and interest claiming his instant attention: there were quaint twisted candlesticks in the shape of snakes, and a teapot fashioned like a china duck, out of whose open beak the tea was supposed to come. How dull and shapeless the nursery teapot seemed in comparison! And there was a carved sandal-wood box packed tight with aromatic cotton-wool, and between the layers of cotton-wool were little brass figures, hump-necked bulls, and peacocks and goblins, delightful to see and to handle. Less promising in appearance was a large square book with plain black covers; Nicholas peeped into it, and, behold, it was full of coloured pictures of birds. And such birds! In the garden, and in the lanes when he went for a walk, Nicholas came across a few birds, of which the largest were an occasional magpie or wood-pigeon; here were herons and bustards, kites, toucans, tiger-bitterns, brush turkeys, ibises, golden pheasants, a whole portrait gallery of undreamed-of creatures. And as he was admiring the colouring of the mandarin duck and assigning a life-history to it, the voice of his aunt in shrill vociferation of his name came from the gooseberry garden without. She had grown suspicious at his long disappearance, and had leapt to the conclusion that he had climbed over the wall behind the sheltering screen of the lilac bushes; she was now engaged in energetic and rather hopeless search for him among the artichokes and raspberry canes.

"Nicholas, Nicholas!" she screamed, "you are to come out of this at once. It's no use trying to hide there; I can see you all the time."

It was probably the first time for twenty years that anyone had smiled in that lumber-room.

Presently the angry repetitions of Nicholas' name gave way to a shriek, and a cry for somebody to come quickly. Nicholas shut the book, restored it carefully to its place in a corner, and shook some dust from a neighbouring pile of newspapers over it. Then he crept from the room, locked the door, and replaced the key exactly where he had found it. His aunt was still calling his name when he sauntered into the front garden.

"Who's calling?" he asked.

"Me," came the answer from the other side of the wall; "didn't you hear me? I've been looking for you in the gooseberry garden, and I've slipped into the rain-water tank. Luckily there's no water in it, but the sides are slippery and I can't get out. Fetch the little ladder from under the cherry tree—"

"I was told I wasn't to go into the gooseberry garden," said Nicholas promptly.

"I told you not to, and now I tell you that you may," came the voice from the rain-water tank, rather impatiently.

"Your voice doesn't sound like aunt's," objected Nicholas; "you may be the Evil One tempting me to be disobedient. Aunt often tells me that the Evil One tempts me and that I always yield. This time I'm not going to yield."

"Don't talk nonsense," said the prisoner in the tank; "go and fetch the ladder."

"Will there be strawberry jam for tea?" asked Nicholas innocently.

"Certainly there will be," said the aunt, privately resolving that Nicholas should have none of it.

"Now I know that you are the Evil One and not aunt," shouted Nicholas gleefully; "when we asked aunt for strawberry jam yesterday she said there wasn't any. I know there are four jars of it in the store cupboard, because I looked, and of course you know it's there, but she doesn't, because she said there wasn't any. Oh, Devil, you *have* sold yourself!"

There was an unusual sense of luxury in being able to talk to an aunt as though one was talking to the Evil One, but Nicholas knew, with childish discernment, that such luxuries were not to be over-indulged in. He walked noisily away, and it was a kitchenmaid, in search of parsley, who eventually rescued the aunt from the rain-water tank.

Tea that evening was partaken of in a fearsome silence. The tide had been at its highest when the children had arrived at Jagborough Cove, so there had been no sands to play on – a circumstance that the aunt had overlooked in the haste of organising her punitive expedition. The tightness of Bobby's boots had had disastrous effect on his temper the whole of the afternoon, and altogether the children could not have been said to have enjoyed themselves. The aunt maintained the frozen muteness of one who has suffered undignified and unmerited detention in a rain-water tank for thirty-five minutes. As for Nicholas, he, too, was silent, in the absorption of one who has much to think about; it was just possible, he considered, that the huntsman would escape with his hounds while the wolves feasted on the stricken stag.

STORY 10

RIP VAN WINKLE

Washington Irving

I

Whoever has made a voyage up the Hudson must remember the Catskill Mountains. They are a branch of the great Appalachian family, and are seen away to the west of the river, swelling up to a noble height, and lording it over the surrounding country. Every change of season, every change of weather, indeed, every hour of the day, produces some change in the magical hues and shapes of these mountains, and they are regarded by all the goodwives, far and near, as perfect barometers.

At the foot of these fairy mountains the traveler may have seen the light smoke curling up from a village, whose shingle roofs gleam among the trees, just where the blue tints of the upland melt away into the fresh green of the nearer landscape. It is a little village of great age, having been founded by some of the Dutch colonists in the early times of the province, just about the beginning of the government of the good Peter Stuyvesant (may he rest in peace!), and there were some of the houses of the original settlers standing within a few years, built of small yellow bricks brought from Holland, having latticed windows and gable fronts, surmounted with weathercocks.

In that same village, and in one of these very houses, there lived, many years since, while the country was yet a province of Great Britain, a simple, good-natured fellow, of the name of Rip Van Winkle. He was a descendant of the Van Winkles who figured so gallantly in the chivalrous days of Peter Stuyvesant, and accompanied him to the siege of Fort Christina. He inherited, however, but little of the martial character of his ancestors. I have observed that he was a simple, good-natured man; he was, moreover, a kind neighbor and an obedient, henpecked husband.

Certain it is that he was a great favorite among all the good-wives of the village, who took his part in all family squabbles; and never failed, whenever they talked those matters over in their evening gossipings, to lay all the blame on Dame Van Winkle. The children of the village, too, would shout with joy whenever he approached. He assisted at their sports, made their playthings, taught them to fly kites and shoot marbles, and told them long stories of ghosts, witches, and Indians. Whenever he went dodging about the village, he was surrounded by a troop of them, hanging on his skirts, clambering on his back, and playing a thousand tricks on him; and not a dog would bark at him throughout the neighborhood.

The great error in Rip's composition was a strong dislike of all kinds of profitable labor. It could not be from the want of perseverance; for he would sit on a wet rock, with a rod as long and heavy as a lance, and fish all day without a murmur, even though he should not be encouraged by a single nibble. He would carry a fowling piece on his shoulder for hours together, trudging through woods and swamps, and uphill and down dale, to shoot a few squirrels or wild pigeons. He would never refuse to assist a neighbor even in the roughest toil, and was a foremost man at all country frolics for husking Indian corn, or building stone fences; the women of the village, too, used to employ him to run their errands, and to do such little odd jobs as their less obliging husbands would not do for them. In a word, Rip was ready to attend to anybody's business but his own; but as to doing family duty, and keeping his farm in order, he found it impossible.

His children, too, were as ragged and wild as if they belonged to nobody. His son Rip promised to inherit the habits, with the old clothes, of his father. He was generally seen trooping like a colt at his mother's heels, equipped in a pair of his father's cast-off breeches, which he had much ado to hold up with one hand, as a fine lady does her train in bad weather.

Rip Van Winkle, however, was one of those happy mortals, of foolish, well-oiled dispositions, who take the world easy, eat white bread or brown, whichever can be got with least thought or trouble, and would rather starve on a penny than work for a pound. If left to himself, he would have whistled life away in perfect contentment; but his wife kept continually dinning in his ear about his idleness, his carelessness, and the ruin he was bringing on his family. Morning, noon, and night, her tongue was incessantly going, and everything he said or did was sure to produce a torrent of household eloquence. Rip had but one way of replying to all lectures of the kind, and that, by frequent use, had grown into a habit. He shrugged his shoulders, shook his head, cast up his eyes, but said nothing. This, however, always provoked a fresh volley from his wife; so that he was fain to draw off his forces, and take to the outside of the house – the only side which, in truth, belongs to a henpecked husband.

Rip's sole domestic adherent was his dog Wolf, who was as much henpecked as his master; for Dame Van Winkle regarded them as companions in idleness, and even looked upon Wolf with an evil eye, as the cause of his master's going so often astray. True it is, in all points of spirit befitting an honorable dog, he was as courageous an animal as ever scoured the woods; but what courage can withstand the ever-enduring and all-besetting terrors of a woman's tongue? The moment Wolf entered the house his crest fell, his tail drooped to the ground or curled between his legs, he sneaked about with a gallows air, casting many a sidelong glance at Dame Van Winkle, and at the least flourish of a broomstick or ladle he would fly to the door with yelping precipitation.

Times grew worse and worse with Rip Van Winkle as years of matrimony rolled on. A tart temper never mellows with age, and a sharp tongue is the only edged tool that grows keener with constant use. For a long while he used to console himself, when driven from home, by frequenting a kind of perpetual club of sages, philosophers, and other idle personages of the village, which held its sessions on a bench before a small inn, designated by a rubicund portrait of His Majesty George III. Here they used to sit in the shade of a long, lazy summer's day, talking listlessly over village gossip, or telling endless sleepy stories about nothing. But it would have been worth any statesman's money to have heard the profound discussions which sometimes took place, when by chance an old newspaper fell into their hands from some passing traveler. How solemnly they would listen to the contents, as drawled out by Derrick Van Bummel, the schoolmaster, — a dapper, learned little man, who was not to be daunted by the most gigantic word in the dictionary! And how sagely they would deliberate upon public events some months after they had taken place!

The opinions of this junto were completely controlled by Nicholas Vedder, a patriarch of the village, and landlord of the inn, at the door of which he took his seat from morning till night, just moving sufficiently to avoid the sun, and keep in the shade of a large tree; so that the neighbors could tell the hour by his movements as accurately as by a sun-dial. It is true, he was rarely heard to speak, but smoked his pipe incessantly. His adherents, however (for every great man has his adherents), perfectly understood him, and knew how to gather his opinions. When anything that was read or related displeased him, he was observed to smoke his pipe vehemently, and to send forth short, frequent, and angry puffs; but, when pleased, he would inhale the smoke slowly and tranquilly, and emit it in light and placid clouds, and sometimes, taking the pipe from his mouth, and letting the fragrant vapor curl about his nose, would nod his head in approbation.

From even this stronghold the unlucky Rip was at length routed by his termagant wife, who would suddenly break in upon the tranquility of the assemblage, and call the members all to naught; nor was that august personage, Nicholas Vedder himself, sacred from the daring tongue of this terrible virago, who charged him with encouraging her husband in habits of idleness.

Poor Rip was at last reduced almost to despair; and his only alternative, to escape from the labor of the farm and clamor of his wife, was to take gun in hand and stroll away into the woods. Here he would sometimes seat himself at the foot of a tree, and share the contents of his wallet with Wolf, with whom he sympathized as a fellow-sufferer in persecution. "Poor Wolf," he would say, "thy mistress leads thee a dog's life of it; but never mind, my lad, whilst I live thou shalt never want a friend to stand by thee."

Wolf would wag his tail, look wistfully in his master's face; and if dogs can feel pity, I verily believe he reciprocated the sentiment with all his heart.

In a long ramble of the kind on a fine autumnal day, Rip had unconsciously scrambled to one of the highest parts of the Catskill Mountains. He was after his favorite sport of squirrel-shooting, and the still solitudes had echoed and reëchoed with the reports of his gun. Panting and fatigued, he threw himself, late in the afternoon, on a green knoll, covered with mountain herbage, that crowned the brow of a precipice. From an opening between the trees he could overlook all the lower country for many a mile of rich woodland. He saw at a distance the lordly Hudson, far, far below him, moving on its silent but majestic course, with the reflection of a purple cloud, or the sail of a lagging bark, here and there sleeping on its glassy bosom, and at last losing itself in the blue highlands.

On the other side he looked down into a deep mountain glen, wild and lonely, the bottom filled with fragments from the overhanging cliffs, and scarcely lighted by the reflected rays of the setting sun. For some time Rip lay musing on this scene; evening was gradually advancing; the mountains began to throw their long blue shadows over the valleys; he saw that it would be dark long before he could reach the village, and he heaved a heavy sigh when he thought of encountering the terrors of Dame Van Winkle.

As he was about to descend, he heard a voice from a distance, hallooing, "Rip Van Winkle! Rip Van Winkle!" He looked round, but could see nothing but a crow winging its solitary flight across the mountain. He thought his fancy must have deceived him, and turned again to descend, when he heard the same cry ring through the still evening air: "Rip Van Winkle! Rip Van Winkle!"

– at the same time Wolf bristled up his back, and giving a low growl, skulked to his master's side, looking fearfully down into the glen. Rip now felt a vague apprehension stealing over him; he looked anxiously in the same direction, and perceived a strange figure slowly toiling up the rocks, and bending under the weight of something he carried on his back. He was surprised to see any human being in this lonely and unfrequented place; but supposing it to be some one of the neighborhood in need of his assistance, he hastened down to yield it.

On nearer approach he was still more surprised at the singularity of the stranger's appearance. He was a short, square-built old fellow, with thick bushy hair, and a grizzled beard. His dress was of the antique Dutch fashion, – a cloth jerkin strapped round the waist, and several pair of breeches, the outer one of ample volume, decorated with rows of buttons down the sides. He bore on his shoulder a stout keg that seemed full of liquor, and made signs for Rip to approach and assist him with the load. Though rather shy and distrustful of this new acquaintance, Rip complied with his usual alacrity, and relieving one another, they clambered up a narrow gully, apparently the dry bed of a mountain torrent.

As they ascended, Rip every now and then heard long, rolling peals, like distant thunder, that seemed to issue out of a deep ravine, or rather cleft, between lofty rocks, toward which their rugged path conducted. He paused for an instant, but supposing it to be the muttering of one of those transient thundershowers which often take place in mountain heights, he proceeded. Passing through the ravine, they came to a hollow, like a small amphitheater, surrounded by perpendicular precipices, over the brinks of which trees shot their branches, so that you only caught glimpses of the azure sky and the bright evening cloud. During the whole time Rip and his companion had labored on in silence; for though the former marveled greatly, what could be the object of carrying a keg of liquor up this wild mountain, yet there was something strange and incomprehensible about the unknown that inspired awe and checked familiarity.

On entering the amphitheater new objects of wonder presented themselves. On a level spot in the center was a company of odd-looking personages playing at ninepins. They were dressed in a quaint, outlandish fashion; some wore short doublets, others jerkins, with long knives in their belts, and most of them had enormous breeches, of similar style with that of the guide's. Their visages, too, were peculiar: one had a large head, broad face, and small, piggish eyes; the face of another seemed to consist entirely of nose, and was surmounted by a white sugar-loaf hat, set off with a little red cock's tail. They all had beards, of various shapes and colors. There was one who seemed to be the commander. He was a stout old gentleman, with a weather-beaten countenance; he wore a laced doublet, broad belt and hanger, high-crowned hat and feather, red stockings, and high-heeled shoes, with roses in them. The whole group reminded Rip of the figures in an old Flemish painting, in the parlor of Dominie Van Shaick, the village parson, which had been brought over from Holland at the time of the settlement.

What seemed particularly odd to Rip was that, though these folks were evidently amusing themselves, yet they maintained the gravest faces, the most mysterious silence, and were, withal, the most melancholy party of pleasure he had ever witnessed. Nothing interrupted the stillness of the scene but the noise of the balls, which, whenever they were rolled, echoed along the mountains like rumbling peals of thunder.

As Rip and his companion approached them, they suddenly desisted from their play, and stared at him with such fixed, statue-like gaze, and such strange, uncouth countenances, that his heart turned within him, and his knees smote together. His companion now emptied the contents of the keg into large flagons, and made signs to him to wait upon the company. He obeyed with fear and trembling; they quaffed the liquor in profound silence, and then returned to their game.

By degrees Rip's awe and apprehension subsided. He even ventured, when no eye was fixed upon him, to taste the beverage, which he found had much of the flavor of excellent Hollands. He was naturally a thirsty soul, and was soon tempted to repeat the draught. One taste provoked another; and he repeated his visits to the flagon so often that at length his senses were overpowered, his eyes swam in his head, his head gradually declined, and he fell into a deep sleep.

II

On waking he found himself on the green knoll whence he had first seen the old man of the glen. He rubbed his eyes – it was a bright, sunny morning. The birds were hopping and twittering among the bushes, and the eagle was wheeling aloft, and breasting the pure mountain breeze. "Surely," thought Rip, "I have not slept here all night." He recalled the occurrences before he fell asleep. The strange man with a keg of liquor – the mountain ravine – the wild retreat among the rocks – the woe-begone party at ninepins – the flagon – "Oh! That flagon! That wicked flagon!" thought Rip; "what excuse shall I make to Dame Van Winkle?"

He looked round for his gun, but in place of the clean, well-oiled fowling piece, he found an old firelock lying by him, the barrel incrusted with rust, the lock falling off, and the stock worm-eaten. He now suspected that the grave revelers of the mountain had put a trick upon him and, having dosed him with liquor, had robbed him of his gun. Wolf, too, had disappeared, but he might have strayed away after a squirrel or partridge. He whistled after him, and shouted his name, but all in vain; the echoes repeated his whistle and shout, but no dog was to be seen.

He determined to revisit the scene of the last evening's gambol, and if he met with any of the party, to demand his dog and gun. As he rose to walk, he found himself stiff in the joints, and wanting in his usual activity. "These mountain beds do not agree with me," thought Rip, "and if this frolic should lay me up with a fit of the rheumatism, I shall have a blessed time with Dame Van Winkle." With some difficulty he got down into the glen; he found the gully up which he and his companion had ascended the preceding evening; but to his astonishment a mountain stream was now foaming down it, leaping from rock to rock, and filling the glen with babbling murmurs. He, however, made shift to scramble up its sides, working his toilsome way through thickets of birch, sassafras, and witch-hazel, and sometimes tripped up or entangled by the wild grapevines that twisted their coils from tree to tree, and spread a kind of network in his path.

At length he reached to where the ravine had opened through the cliffs to the amphitheater; but no traces of such opening remained. The rocks presented a high, impenetrable wall, over which the torrent came tumbling in a sheet of feathery foam, and fell into a broad, deep basin, black from the shadows of the surrounding forest. Here, then, poor Rip was brought to a stand.

He again called and whistled after his dog; he was only answered by the cawing of a flock of idle crows sporting high in air about a dry tree that overhung a sunny precipice; and who, secure in their elevation, seemed to look down and scoff at the poor man's perplexities. What was to be done? – The morning was passing away, and Rip felt famished for want of his breakfast. He grieved to give up his dog and gun; he dreaded to meet his wife; but it would not do to starve among the mountains. He shook his head, shouldered the rusty firelock, and, with a heart full of trouble and anxiety, turned his steps homeward.

As he approached the village he met a number of people, but none whom he knew, which somewhat surprised him, for he had thought himself acquainted with everyone in the country round. Their dress, too, was of a different fashion from that to which he was accustomed. They all stared at him with equal marks of surprise, and whenever they cast their eyes upon him, invariably stroked their chins. The constant recurrence of this gesture induced Rip, involuntarily, to do the same, when, to his astonishment, he found his beard had grown a foot long!

He had now entered the skirts of the village. A troop of strange children ran at his heels, hooting after him, and pointing at his gray beard. The dogs, too, not one of which he recognized for an old acquaintance, barked at him as he passed. The very village was altered; it was larger and more populous. There were rows of houses which he had never seen before, and those which had been his familiar haunts had disappeared. Strange names were over the doors – strange faces at the windows – everything was strange. His mind now misgave him; he began to doubt whether both he and the world around him were not bewitched. Surely this was his native village, which he had left but the day before. There stood the Catskill Mountains – there ran the silver

Hudson at a distance – there was every hill and dale precisely as it had always been. Rip was sorely perplexed. "That flagon last night," thought he, "has addled my poor head sadly!"

It was with some difficulty that he found the way to his own house, which he approached with silent awe, expecting every moment to hear the shrill voice of Dame Van Winkle. He found the house gone to decay – the roof fallen in, the windows shattered, and the doors off the hinges. A half-starved dog that looked like Wolf was skulking about it. Rip called him by name, but the cur snarled, showed his teeth, and passed on. This was an unkind cut indeed. "My very dog," sighed Rip, "has forgotten me!"

He entered the house, which, to tell the truth, Dame Van Winkle had always kept in neat order. It was empty, forlorn, and apparently abandoned. He called loudly for his wife and children – the lonely chambers rang for a moment with his voice, and then all again was silence.

III

He now hurried forth, and hastened to his old resort, the village inn – but it, too, was gone. A large, rickety wooden building stood in its place, with great gaping windows, some of them broken and mended with old hats and petticoats, and over the door was painted, "The Union Hotel, by Jonathan Doolittle." Instead of the great tree that used to shelter the quiet little Dutch inn of yore, there now was reared a tall, naked pole, with something on the top that looked like a red nightcap, and from it was fluttering a flag, on which was a singular assemblage of stars and stripes; all this was strange and incomprehensible. He recognized on the sign, however, the ruby face of King George, under which he had smoked so many a peaceful pipe; but even this was singularly changed. The red coat was changed for one of blue and buff, a sword was held in the hand instead of a scepter, the head was decorated with a cocked hat, and underneath was painted in large characters, GENERAL WASHINGTON.

There was, as usual, a crowd of folk about the door, but none that Rip recollected. The very character of the people seemed changed. There was a busy, bustling tone about it, instead of the accustomed drowsy tranquility. He looked in vain for the sage Nicholas Vedder, with his broad face, double chin, and long pipe, uttering clouds of tobacco smoke instead of idle speeches; or Van Bummel, the schoolmaster, doling forth the contents of an ancient newspaper. In place of these, a lean fellow, with his pockets full of handbills, was haranguing vehemently about rights of citizens – elections – members of congress – Bunker's Hill – heroes of seventy-six – and other words, which were a perfect jargon to the bewildered Van Winkle.

The appearance of Rip, with his long, grizzled beard, his rusty fowling piece, his uncouth dress, and an army of women and children at his heels, soon attracted the attention of the tavern politicians. They crowded round him, eyeing him from head to foot with great curiosity. The orator bustled up to him, and, drawing him partly aside, inquired "On which side he voted?" Rip stared in vacant stupidity. Another short but busy little fellow pulled him by the arm, and, rising on tiptoe, inquired in his ear, "Whether he was Federal or Democrat?" Rip was equally at a loss to comprehend the question; when a knowing, self-important old gentleman, in a sharp cocked hat, made his way through the crowd, putting them to the right and left with his elbows as he passed, and planting himself before Van Winkle, with one arm akimbo, the other resting on his cane, his keen eyes and sharp hat penetrating, as it were, into his very soul, demanded, in an austere tone, "What brought him to the election with a gun on his shoulder, and a mob at his heels; and whether he meant to breed a riot in the village?" – "Alas! Gentlemen," cried Rip, somewhat dismayed, "I am a poor, quiet man, a native of the place, and a loyal subject of the king, God bless him!"

Here a general shout burst from the bystanders – "A tory! A tory! A spy! A refugee! Hustle him! Away with him!" It was with great difficulty that the self-important man in the cocked hat restored order; and having assumed a tenfold austerity of brow, demanded again of the unknown culprit, what he came there for, and whom he was seeking! The poor man humbly assured him that he meant no harm, but merely came there in search of some of his neighbors.

"Well – who are they? Name them."

Rip bethought himself a moment, and inquired, "Where's Nicholas Vedder?"

There was a silence for a little while, when an old man replied, in a thin, piping voice, "Nicholas Vedder! Why, he is dead and gone these eighteen years! There was a wooden tombstone in the churchyard that used to tell all about him, but that's rotten and gone, too."

"Where's Brom Dutcher?"

"Oh, he went off to the army in the beginning of the war; some say he was killed at the storming of Stony Point; others say he was drowned in a squall at the foot of Anthony's Nose. I don't know; he never came back again."

"Where's Van Brummel, the schoolmaster?"

"He went off to the wars, too, was a great militia general, and is now in congress."

Rip's heart died away at hearing of these sad changes in his home and friends and finding himself thus alone in the world.

Every answer puzzled him, too, by treating of such enormous lapses of time, and of matters which he could not understand: war – congress – Stony Point. He had no courage to ask after any more friends, but cried out in despair, "Does nobody here know Rip Van Winkle?"

"Oh, Rip Van Winkle!" exclaimed two or three, "oh, to be sure! That's Rip Van Winkle yonder, leaning against the tree."

Rip looked, and beheld a precise counterpart of himself, as he went up the mountain – apparently as lazy and certainly as ragged. The poor fellow was now completely confounded. He doubted his own identity, and whether he was himself or another man. In the midst of his bewilderment, the man in the cocked hat demanded who he was, and what was his name.

"God knows," exclaimed he, at his wits' end; "I'm not myself – I'm somebody else – that's me yonder – no – that's somebody else got into my shoes – I was myself last night, but I fell asleep on the mountain, and they've changed my gun, and everything's changed, and I'm changed, and I can't tell what's my name, or who I am!"

The bystanders began now to look at each other, nod, wink significantly, and tap their fingers against their foreheads. There was a whisper, also, about securing the gun, and keeping the old fellow from doing mischief, at the very suggestion of which the self-important man in the cocked hat retired with some precipitation. At this critical moment a fresh, comely woman pressed through the throng to get a peep at the gray-bearded man. She had a chubby child in her arms, which, frightened at his looks, began to cry. "Hush, Rip," cried she, "hush, you little fool; the old man won't hurt you." The name of the child, the air of the mother, the tone of her voice, all awakened a train of recollections in his mind. "What is your name, my good woman?" asked he.

"Judith Gardenier."

"And your father's name?"

"Ah, poor man, Rip Van Winkle was his name, but it's twenty years since he went away from home with his gun, and never has been heard of since – his dog came home without him; but whether he shot himself, or was carried away by the Indians, nobody can tell. I was then but a little girl."

Rip had but one question more to ask; but he put it with a faltering voice:

"Where's your mother?"

"Oh, she, too, had died but a short time since; she broke a blood-vessel in a fit of passion at a New England peddler."

There was a drop of comfort, at least, in this intelligence. The honest man could contain himself no longer. He caught his daughter and her child in his arms. "I am your father!" cried he – "Young Rip Van Winkle once – Old Rip Van Winkle now! Does nobody know poor Rip Van Winkle?"

All stood amazed until an old woman, tottering out from among the crowd, put her hand to her brow, and peering under it in his face for a moment, exclaimed, "Sure enough! It is Rip Van Winkle – it is himself! Welcome home again, old neighbor. Why, where have you been these twenty long years?"

Rip's story was soon told, for the whole twenty years had been to him but as one night. The neighbors stared when they heard it; some were seen to wink at each other, and put their tongues in their cheeks: and the self-important man in the cocked hat, who when the alarm was over had returned to the field, screwed down the corners of his mouth, and shook his head – upon which there was a general shaking of the head throughout the assemblage.

It was determined, however, to take the opinion of old Peter Vanderdonk, who was seen slowly advancing up the road. He was a descendant of the historian of that name, who wrote one of the earliest accounts of the province. Peter was the most ancient inhabitant of the village, and well versed in all the wonderful events and traditions of the neighborhood. He recollected Rip at once, and corroborated his story in the most satisfactory manner. He assured the company that it was a fact, handed down from his ancestor the historian, that the Catskill Mountains had always been haunted by strange beings. It was affirmed that the great Hendrick Hudson, the first discoverer of the river and country, kept a kind of vigil there every twenty years, with his crew of the *Half-moon*; being permitted in this way to revisit the scenes of his enterprise, and keep a guardian eye upon the river and the great city called by his name. His father had once seen them in their old Dutch dresses playing at ninepins in a hollow of the mountain; and he himself had heard, one summer afternoon, the sound of their balls, like distant peals of thunder.

To make a long story short, the company broke up and returned to the more important concerns of the election. Rip's daughter took him home to live with her; she had a snug, well-furnished house, and a stout, cheery farmer for a husband, whom Rip recollected for one of the urchins that used to climb upon his back. As to Rip's son and heir, who was the ditto of himself, seen leaning against the tree, he was employed to work on the farm; but showed a hereditary disposition to attend to anything else but his business.

OTHER BOOKS YOU MAY LIKE

- 12 Years a Slave by Solomon Northup, ISBN: 9789390492374
- 51 Most Powerful Prayers by Ryan, ISBN: 9789354990847
- A Christmas Carol by Charles Dickens, ISBN: 9788193545874
- A Cloud by Day, a Fire by Night by AW Tozer, ISBN: 9789354990854
- A Streetcar Named Desire by Tennessee Williams, ISBN: 9788194748601
- Abraham Lincoln by Lord Charnwood, ISBN: 9789380914251
- Absolute Surrender by Andrew Murray, ISBN: 9789389716269
- Annihilation of Caste by Dr B.R. Ambedkar, ISBN: 9789390492732
- Awakened Imagination by Neville Goddard, ISBN: 9789389157086
- Be What You Wish by Neville Goddard, ISBN: 9789387669550
- Believe in Yourself by Joseph Murphy, ISBN: 9789388118385
- Chanakya Neeti by Chanakya, ISBN: 9789389716276
- Civilization and Its Discontents by Sigmund Freud, ISBN: 9789387669499
- Delighting in God by AW Tozer, ISBN: 9788194748632
- Experiencing the Holy Spirit by Andrew Murray, ISBN: 9788194764809
- Feeling is the Secret by Neville Goddard, ISBN: 9789389157109
- George Orwell Combo : Animal Farm & 1984, ISBN: 9789390492459
- Gravity by George Gamow, ISBN: 9789388118484
- Guerrilla Warfare by Ernesto Che Guevara, ISBN: 9789354990366
- How I Made $2 Million in the Stock Market by N. Darvas, ISBN: 9789389716283
- How to Attract Money by Joseph Murphy, ISBN: 9789388118408
- How to be filled with the Holy Spirit by AW Tozer, ISBN: 9789389157116
- How to Develop Self Confidence by Dale Carnegie, ISBN: 9789387669000
- How to Enjoy Your Life and Your Job by Dale Carnegie, ISBN: 9789387669017
- How to Stop Worrying and Start Living by Dale Carnegie, ISBN: 9789380914817
- How to Win Friends and Influence People by D. Carnegie, ISBN: 9788180320217

Develop your reading habit | **Gift books to your friends**

OTHER BOOKS YOU MAY LIKE

- In His Steps by Charles M. Sheldon, ISBN: 9789390492794
- Jail Diary and Other Writings by Bhagat Singh, ISBN: 9789390492398
- Know Your Worth by NK Sondhi & Vibha Malhotra, ISBN: 9788180320231
- Life of Christ by Fulton J. Sheen, ISBN: 9789389716306
- Man: The Dwelling Place of God by AW Tozer, ISBN: 9789354990656
- Maneaters of Kumaon by Jim Corbett, ISBN: 9789354990731
- Mansarover 2 (Hindi) by Premchand, ISBN: 9789380914985
- Meditation and Its Methods by Swami Vivekananda, ISBN: 9789389716320
- Meditations by Marcus Aurelius, ISBN: 9789388118736
- My Experiments with Truth by Mahatma Gandhi, ISBN: 9789387669291
- My Inventions: The Autobiography of Nikola Tesla, ISBN: 9789388118132
- Paths to Power by AW Tozer, ISBN: Forthcoming
- Relativity by Albert Einstein, ISBN: 9789380914220
- Reminiscences of a Stock Operator by Edwin Lefevre, ISBN: 9788194764816
- Scientific Healing Affirmations by P. Yogananda, ISBN: 9789389716344
- Selected Stories of Rabindranath Tagore by Tagore, ISBN: 9789380914770
- Student's Encyclopedia of G. K. by GP Editors, ISBN: 9789380914190
- Success Through a Positive Mental Attitude by N. Hill, ISBN: 9789390492435
- The Alchemy of Happiness by Al-Ghazzali, ISBN: 9789387669505
- The Art of War by Sun Tzu, ISBN: 9789380914893
- The Autobiography of a Yogi by Paramahansa Yogananda, ISBN: 9789380914602
- The Book of Enoch by Enoch, ISBN: 9789390492480
- The Diary of a Young Girl by Anne Frank, ISBN: 9789380914312
- The Dynamic Laws of Prosperity by Catherine Ponder, ISBN: 9789388118156
- The Elements of Style by William Strunk, ISBN: 9789389157123
- The Game of Life and How to Play It by Florence Shinn, ISBN: 9789387669390

Develop your reading habit | **Gift books to your friends**

OTHER BOOKS YOU MAY LIKE

- The Imitation of Christ by Thomas À Kempis, ISBN: 9789388118057
- The Knowledge of the Holy by AW Tozer, ISBN: 9789389157130
- The Law by Neville Goddard, ISBN: 9789390492886
- The Law of Success by Napoleon Hill, ISBN: 9788180320927
- The Light of Asia by Sir Edwin Arnold, ISBN: 9789380914923
- The Magic of Believing by Claudie Bristol, ISBN: 9789388118149
- The Magic of Faith by Joseph Murphy, ISBN: 9789388118743
- The Miracles of Your Mind by Joseph Murphy, ISBN: 9788180320743
- The Origin of Species by Charles Darwin, ISBN: 9788180320453
- The Power of Awareness by Neville Goddard, ISBN: 9789387669406
- The Power of Positive Thinking by Norman Vincent Peale, ISBN: 9789388118569
- The Power of Your Subconscious Mind by Joseph Murphy, ISBN: 9788180320958
- The Problem of Increasing Human Energy by Nikola Tesla, ISBN: 9789354990953
- The Psychopathology of Everyday Life by Sigmund Freud, ISBN: 9789388118071
- The Pursuit of God by AW Tozer, ISBN: 9789389157147
- The Red Badge of Courage by Stephen Crane, ISBN: 9789354990977
- The Richest Man in Babylon by George S. Clason, ISBN: 9789387669369
- The Science of Getting Rich by Wallace D. Wattles, ISBN: 9788180320972
- The World as I See It by Albert Einstein, ISBN: 9789388118125
- The Yoga Sutras of Patanjali by Patanjali, ISBN: 9789389716351
- Think and Grow Rich by Napoleon Hill, ISBN: 9788180320255
- Thought Vibration by William Walker Atkinson, ISBN: 9789389157154
- Who were the Shudras by Dr B.R. Ambedkar, ISBN: 9789354991028
- Wuthering Heights by Emily Brontë, ISBN: 9788193545898
- Your Faith is Your Fortune by Neville Goddard, ISBN: 9789389157161
- Zen in the Art of Archery by Eugen Herrigel, ISBN: 9789354991059

Develop your reading habit | **Gift books to your friends**